Lust stories

Season 1

By

Rajveer Shekhawat

Also from the authors

wife swapping: All Episodes Editions Kindle Edition

wife swapping: All Episodes Editions Paperback – Large Print, April 6, 2020

Social media connectivity

INSTAGRAM@ DEAD_OF_WRITE27

@ INK_AND_FABLES27

@ VINTAGE_QUOTES_WORDS

TWITTER@ BHASKAR_PANDEY

Contents

I got fucked by friend's father-in-law

Hello friends, my name is Anisha. I belong to a small village. In-laws are cultivated, but all people live in the city. Sometimes people from our family come to their village. Some farming work is done. The village also has a sex story, I will tell you later.

By the way, I have already told you my figure size. For new friends, I am telling my figure of 34-28-36 again. I am very beautiful to watch.

A few days after the wedding, we took a separate house for rent in the city itself. There was some problem in our house. There was less space because this also had to take another house. From this new house, my husband used to get very close to coming to the office. My husband used to live outside more than work.

A few days after moving to this new house, I met Vanita, a neighbour living on my side. In a few days, we both became good friends too.

Only my husband and I lived in my house. Apart from her husband and father-in-law, there was also a boy in Vanita's house. Vanita's mother-in-law was no longer in this world.

Vanita is 26 years old and her figure is also 34-26-36 like mine. Its weight will be around 54 kg and height is 5 feet 3 inches. She was beautiful to look at.

We used to stay in the house in the afternoon, either Vanita would come to my house or I would go to her house. We both slowly started talking freely. The colour of sex was beginning to solidify in our talks. We both used to discuss openly sex. What happened before marriage and who was still having an affair after marriage. Which girl is having an affair with the surrounding area… etcetera.

Then I also met Vanita's father-in-law. He used to talk to me a little bit. Like he would ask how are you eating or not… etc.

Then my husband's identity also became good with Vanita's father-in-law Rajendra Kumar. Rajendra Kumar also started coming to my house. The special thing is that Rajendra, father-in-law of Vanita, was a very cheerful person. He was always in a joking mood. Due to his nature, he started joking with me and my husband too.

One day I was at home and Vanita went out of
work. His father-in-law Rajendra Kumar Ji went out.
So I had the key to his house.

Rajendra Kumar, the father-in-law of Vanita, came
to my house at around 12:30. They rang the
doorbell, I was washing clothes at that time. My
salwar was half wet. Then I hurried and opened the
door without an odour.

Rajendra Kumar was in front. He smiled and came
to my house.
He asked - what was Anu doing?
I said - I was washing clothes. You sit, I come now.

I did not even think that they were looking at my
mother. I started cleaning clothes and talking too.
Then I realized that they are seeing my mother
moving.
By then my work was done, so I cleaned my hands
and started giving them water.

On the pretext of taking water, his hands touched
my hand. Rajendra Ji took a glass of water from my
hand and started drinking water. By then Vanita
also came. They both went to their home. I too
came to the hall after doing all my work and turned
on the TV and started watching the serial.

After some time the doorbell rang again. When I
opened the door, there was Vanita in front. She

came in and sat near me and started watching TV.
We both started talking while watching TV.

I asked about things, man, Vanita, how much time
has your mother-in-law passed?
So she said - it's been almost 3 years… Why are
you asking?
I said - I am asking just like this, by the way, you
take very good care of father-in-law Rajendra Ji.
She said yes man, have to keep it.

I fell silent.

Then she said, man, I wanted to ask one thing.
I said - ask yes!
So bid - man, I think you were looking at my
father-in-law too much.
I said no man… there was nothing like that.
Vanita said- Hmm, don't tell a lie, tell me one thing,
my father-in-law is mad at you.
I said - how is that?
So bid - man, you are young, beautiful… and when
I came to get the key, the door was open,
father-in-law was taking a glass of water in hand. At
that time, his eyes were on your Milky Moms.
I bid no man.
So they bid - Ok, let's try and see what happens.

I jokingly agreed to him. Then she sat for some
time and went to her house.

After this, I started checking this thing in front of Rajendraji. If they used to come to my house, I would sometimes bow down in front of them and start sweeping; Also, I used to look in front of them secretly, they would always keep looking at my boobs and ass.

It has been two months like this.

Then once the husband had to go out of his work at night for three weeks. Then there was also the birthday of Vanita's son. He also called both of us.

On the same day, the husband had to go out, so he said - you go to the hotel, I will take some gift and give it there.
The husband left around six o'clock.

The birthday party was in a hotel at night, food was also kept in it. If a lot of people wanted to come to the party, then I started getting ready to leave. I wore a red coloured saree and remembering my father-in-law, I wore a deep-necked blouse, this blouse was completely open from the back, out of which my back looked very naked. I kept looking at myself in the mirror and smiled. Out of this blouse, my mamma was going to come out.

Then Vanita came to call me and looking at me, she said, "Wow ... You are looking very good ... It

seems that today my father-in-law will be made crazy."
I also smiled at her.

After that, I locked the house and left.
We all came out in the evening at 7:30. Vanita and Vanita's husband Rajendra Ji and another guest got out of the Swift car. The guests sat in the car ahead. Vanita, I and Rajendra were in the back seat. Vanita was on the window seat. Father in law sat on my side. When the car came on the highway, Rajendraji's elbow started touching my mother. Vanita was sitting with her legs spread deliberately. With which I stuck with Vanita's father-in-law even more. Therefore, he got more opportunity.

I didn't say anything because of his elbow. So he dared to suppress my mother slowly. Now I too started having fun.
We reached the hotel in a while.

Then my husband got a call, he said - where are you guys?
I told them - we are in the Monarch Hotel.
He said - ok I am coming too.

After some time, the husband arrived with a gift. After that, we all cut the cake and had a small party. After the party, we all reached home at night. It was 10:30 then.

The car was not already in place. That's why the
husband said - You guys leave, I come.

Then likewise, he sat in the car and started coming
home. So this time Rajendra Ji started his work
while sitting in the car and started moving his hands
on my navel. I held his hand and saw him, then he
stopped a little. Then after a couple of minutes,
they started touching my mother. My pussy was in
bad shape.

I started pressing his hand by hand. When Vanita
looked at me, she smiled.

We came home at some time. I came down later.

Rajendraji said the most - Come on you guys, I
bring some stuff.

He also told me to stop. Giving my mobile phone
slowly in my hand, he said - look at the battery.

Everyone went home without thinking about
anything. Then Rajendra Ji held my hand and
kissed me, looking very hot and sexy.
I blushed and said - I will leave. Someone will see.

On arrival at home, her husband also reached
home. I removed the sari and wore a nightie. That
night my husband once fucking me and went out.

I started thinking about Vanita's father-in-law Rajendra Ji and started fingering my thirsty pussy.

Once I got a lot of juice out of my pussy. Then I fell asleep.

My husband got a call in the morning that he would come back today. Their work was not done and the program to stay for three weeks was cancelled.

After talking to my husband, I looked at myself fresh. By around 12:00 I had finished all my work. Then someone rang the doorbell. When I opened the door, there was Rajendraji in front. He smiled and came in and started asking about my husband. I said that he had gone out at night. But it will come by this evening.

By now I had closed the door. I bid - make tea for you.

I went to the kitchen. That day I was wearing a leggie and was wearing a fitted top. My figure was clearly visible in this dress. I made tea and brought them.
He said while drinking tea - if we had milk, he would have enjoyed it.
I quote - Okay, bring it now.

So while holding my hand, Rajendra said - don't drink that milk, give me your milk, my queen.

Rajendraji pulled me on his lap and kissed me on
my cheeks.

I let them kiss me. They were about to move further
than I stopped them.

I said - Uncle Ji, not now… give me some more
time… after that, we will all do it.
He too agreed and while suppressing my mother,
said - Ok… but I will kiss every day.
I filled us - OK.

They left after some time.

Vanita arrived an hour later. She started asking
about the car.

Then I said - yes, I was enjoying it.
She said - okay what happened today?

I told him all that Uncle did, suppressed Mmmm…
et cetera.

So Vanita said- Oh God… Now when I go out
tomorrow, call them to your house and tell me all
what they do next.
I laughed and said - OK.

Then the next day Vanita went out of work in the
morning. I was also alone from 12 noon to 2 that
day. Husband left the office in the morning.

As soon as Vanita left, her father-in-law came to me. I kept the door open. I knew that Rajendra Ji would come to me as soon as Vanita left.

This is what happened… He came to my house as soon as Vanita left. He closed the door.

I was in the kitchen, they came there and started kissing me.
Then I said - Uncle, walk in the hall, I come there.

On the second day, Vanita went out of work in the morning. I was also alone from 12 noon to 2 that day. Husband left the office in the morning.

As soon as Vanita left, her father-in-law came to me. I kept the door open. I knew that Rajendra Ji would come to me as soon as Vanita left.

This is what happened… He came to my house as soon as Vanita left. He closed the door.
I was in the kitchen, they came there and started kissing me.
Then I said - Uncle, walk in the hall, I come there.

Father in law came to the hall.

After Rajendra uncle left, I also came into the hall and sat on his arm. Father in law started kissing me.

I started asking him - Uncle, how did you get such a
dirty idea about me?
He said - When you will shake me and see your
backyard, then what will I do... no one will follow
you.

Then we both talked for a while. Then Vanita's call
came. She said - I am coming to your house, where
his father in law is.
I said loudly on the phone - Yes, they are at my
house.

he hung up.

When Rajendra looked at me, I told him that Vanita
had a call and she is coming here only. She was
asking about you.
He recovered and set me apart.

It went on like this for a few days.

Then one day the husband had to go out of work,
then the husband called me and said - keep my
bag ready, I have to go to Chennai in the evening, it
will take at least 15 days.
I cut the phone saying OK and started keeping the
husband's luggage in the bag.

Then Vanita came and looked at the bag, bid - it
seems, you are going somewhere.
I said no man... husband is going out of work.

Vanita said- Wao yaar… when are you going?
I bid - tonight.
That quote - Ok…

We both talked for a while and she left.

At night, the husband came and had some rest
after having food and at 11 o'clock they left. That
night I slept alone.

The next day Vanita came home in the afternoon
and started asking me when did her husband
leave?
I bid - 11 o'clock at night.
Then she said - tonight I will send it to my
father-in-law.
I smiled. I said - Hey friend, what will your husband
think?
So she said nothing, I will talk… and you have
dinner at my house tonight.
I said - OK, but tell me what is your benefit in this?
She said - I will tell them all later.

She left me with a wink.

I went to her house at night. I wore the same red
sari and blouse again today.
Rajendraji, the father-in-law of Vanita, looked at me
and said - how are you?
I am very slow.

Then Vanita came and said to me - Let's have
dinner.

We all sat down to eat. Vanita said while eating
food- Babuji, can you go to Anisha's house to sleep
today? He is scared to sleep alone.

Vanita's father-in-law Rajendra immediately agreed.
As soon as I had food, I started distributing Vanita's
little hand in covering the vessel.

Vanita said- Man, leave it all, go and have fun
today.
I laughed and said - OK.

I came to my house. Rajendra Ji also followed me. I
closed the door and entered the bedroom.
As soon as I went there, Uncle Ji filled me in the
arms and started kissing. At the same time, they
started suppressing my mother.

I did - let me change the saree.
So said - No… Change what to do… It will go down
now.

He started kissing me on the bed. He slowly took
off my blouse. I did not know when my saree
landed. I also removed his shirt. I started kissing
them by lying under them. When his Bermuda
landed, his black cock of 8 was asleep.

I started sucking Uncle's cock with my hand.

They too became ready in two minutes. Then he started fingering my pussy. As soon as the finger of a foreign man in the pussy went, my sobriety started coming out. I started doing 'Uhu… Ahaha ..'.

Rajendraji, the father-in-law of Vanita, kissed me while lying down and said while pressing my moms - you are a very good thing, my life… The whole neighbourhood wants to fuck you.

They climbed on top of me. His cocks which were 8 inches asleep, he was now feeling full of hands. Uncle set his pestle and set it in my pussy. Slowly, while looking at me, I started putting my cock in my pussy. I was also supporting Uncle. As soon as half of their cocks went in, my eyes started expanding. I had not taken such a big cock till today.

Then Uncle gave a sharp push and licked his entire cock in my pussy. I screamed But uncle paid no attention to my scream and started fucking me loudly. The sounds of my 'Ummah… Ahhh… Hah… Yah…' started echoing in the bedroom.

After about five minutes, my pussy set Uncle's cock inside me and I started to enjoy fucking Chick with Uncle.

I fell twice during a ten-minute quick fuck. Then
Uncle also left his semen in my pussy.

This is how I got my first fuck with a non-male.

Then we both started talking to each other nakedly.

I said - how was my pussy?
So he said - Mast... looked very tight. Does your
husband not fuck you properly?
I said yes.
Then Uncle said - I love fucking women on the ass.
I bid - as you like, you fuck me.

Then after some time, he turned 69. Kissing me in
the thighs started licking my pussy and Uncle gave
his cock in my mouth.

As soon as Uncle's cock stood up, he told me to be
a bitch. I quickly became a dog. Uncle started
slapping my ass very hard. I was in a lot of pain
with their moons. He made my ass red by slapping
it. Along with that, my mummies also mashed them
out loud and turned completely red.

After that, in the bitch pose, I fitted the cocks from
behind me and while pressing my mummies, licked
the cocks in my pussy loudly. I was completely
pained by his cocks and I started crying.

But he did not agree and started fucking me loudly.
After some time I too started having fun. While
shaking my ass, I started taking his cock inside.

In this way, Vanita's father-in-law fucks my pussy 3
times in the night. After enjoying sex all night, both
of us slept at 4 in the morning. Then Uncle went up
at seven in the morning. But I was able to wake up
at 11 o'clock.

When I saw the day, Vanita had many missed calls.
I had picked up the phone that his phone came
again.

He told me - man, take a bath with Babuji.
I bid OK.

Then Vanita's father-in-law also came.

He said - I was going to take a bath, then thought I
would wake you up.
So I said - OK you stop here, now we both take
baths together.

They also agreed. The two of us entered the
washroom together.

My ass and mummies were still red due tonight
cuddles and uncle's moons.

Vanita's father-in-law while taking a bath said - Anu enjoyed?
I kissed him and said - I enjoyed it.
Did he say - then today?
I said - you will stay with me every day until the husband comes. You will fuck me every day.
He laughed and said - Hey, I liked my cock… My darling, I will make you happy by fucking me in every way.

Then Uncle, looking at my mother, said that he is looking for cool red tomatoes and today I will also put cocks in the ass.
I bid OK.

We bathed and refreshed and made tea.

Vanita came to my house as soon as Rajendra uncle left. She said wow man, you are looking very beautiful today.
I smiled and told him everything that happened with Uncle in the night.

That quote - Wow Mast… Now I want to see your and Babuji's fuck.
I said - how is that?
So she said - in the afternoon.

I felt a little strange, so she said - you keep the door open in the afternoon, I will come.

I thought maybe Vanita would want to take her
father-in-law's cock, so she wants to see his cock.

In the afternoon, the uncle came back to my house.
I laughed and said - did not have patience?
Vanita's father-in-law said - You are such a thing.
I told my father-in-law what to do.
Father-in-law… you close the door, I go to the
room.

I closed the door but did not latch inside. We were
kissing in the room that Vanita came and showered
on her father-in-law.

She started scolding me too. I was shocked and
silent. Vanita's father-in-law was apologizing to
Vanita.
Vanita said- Babuji is fine, but you will have to do
one of my work as well.
He said - what?
Then Vanita said - Babuji I want to go round with
your friend Ravindra.
He said with surprise - what?
Vanita said- Yes Babuji.
He too agreed and said- Bahu, although he will
agree, but how can I speak to him?
Vanita said- Babuji, when he comes home, you just
go out, I will take care of the work ahead.
He said - okay.

Then Vanita came on my side and said -
Implemented mother-in-law.
Rajendra Ji also smiled.
Vanita said- OK Babu Ji, how is my friend's test?
So he said - he is cool.

I told uncle - you come at night.
He will come at night.

Uncle went away. Even though Vanita did not stop,
she also left.

They both went away speaking the night. Then
Vanita started talking openly with her father-in-law
too. Vanita's meeting with her father-in-law was
done with Ravindra.

Vanita got set for four days with Ravindra. He first
told me as soon as he was set with Ravindra. Then
he also told his father-in-law.

So far, my mother-in-law and mother-in-law are
enjoying the law said - My sister-in-law, my
sister-in-law came out even faster than me.
Ravindra was set.

Then Ravindra and Vanita's fuck program was also
decided to be in my own house.

For this, Vanita's father-in-law sent her son to Bua's
house for 2 days with some work. Vanita had

already told Ravindra that her husband was about to go out.

She was going to come to my house to sleep that night. Therefore, he told Ravindra that you should come there at night.

She came alone in the night. I said to Vanita - where have you come alone? What do I have to do?
She said yes man, he is going to come. Tonight just you go to my house. Have fun with your father in law.

Ravindra also came to my house at that time. He said to me - where are you going to sleep?
I bid - here in the hall.

Those people went to my bedroom.

Did not sleep that night Anisha started listening to the sounds of her friend Vanita and Ravindra's fucking.
Vanita said - Speak slowly, my friend is outside.
He said - did not do anything yet.

They started kissing Vanita and they both started undressing each other on the bed.

Ravindra started fingering Vanita's pussy.
Vanita said - Babuji should not know.

He said - no my love.

He started kissing Vanita. I was watching
everything from outside. The bedroom door was
open. Seeing their fuck, I started getting itchy in my
pussy too.

Vanita started caressing Ravindra's 7-inch thick
cock. Ravindra also started fingering Vanita's
pussy.

After some time both of them started fucking.
Fucking lasted for about 15 minutes. After that,
both of them fell and lay bare like that.

I also fell asleep with my finger in my pussy. That
night, Vanita's father-in-law kept waiting for me, she
was strong. Due to Ravindra, he could not come to
my house. I also turned off my mobile.
Because of this, I had to become a victim of
Vanita's father-in-law's cocks from morning to
morning. On that day, Uncle ate me for an hour
continuously, after eating medicine, my pussy was
swollen with uncle's hand by hand. After he left, I
forced my pussy for an hour with hot water. It was a
privilege that Uncle did not accept my ass.

That night, Ravindra had stabbed Vanita 3 times.
How was that fuck, when Vanita will tell me?

Goodbye till then.

I was troubled by my sex story

Friends, I am your dear friend Preeti Sharma, Today I have brought you my completely new experience. While I was writing this story, my hands were still shivering. A strange adventure, a strange sensation is running all over my body. So take it, read my past.

One day I was sitting empty like that, so I thought about what to do. First I read sexy stories consciously, after reading a couple of hot stories, my pussy got erect.

Now you will say, man what the fuck is she doing, Lulli stands up, cocks stand up, how can her sister-in-law stand up. Listen to me carefully, when you will read this story completely, then you will also know that pussy also stands up. Not everyone, but there is a woman whose pussy is erect, I have seen, so I am telling you.

So after reading a couple of stories when my panty got wet with my puddle water, I got up and went to the kitchen, there I opened the fridge and started looking for something inside, then I saw a cucumber, I picked that cucumber and went to the bathroom. I went there, I took off all my clothes and then after putting it on the side of the leg, I took that cucumber in my skin.

When the cucumber was cold, it numbed my fudge inside. But I was very hot, after seeing my naked body in large glass in front of me, I started making cucumber in my hair. My pace and fun both started increasing. And then came to know only when the white coloured water fell from my clit and my anus reached my feet through the smooth thighs.

Even after falling water, I stood with my cucumber in the same way for some time. Shortly after the water receded, when my puddle became completely cold, I bathed first and then came out wearing new clothes.

When I came back, I saw my husband Deepak, sitting on my laptop recently. His face turned red with anger upon seeing me. Seeing my laptop in his hand, my ass was torn, man, he knew all my exploits.

Before I could say something, they had to bifurcate - how long has all this been going on?

Of course, Deepak has never been angry with me
till today, but for the first time today, I was very
scared to see his anger. What would I answer?

He then roared - and who is this Varinder Singh
who writes stories for you. Is your mother even
more than this?
Tears came out of my eyes.
I said with a hug, please listen to me, I have no
problem with anyone, they only write stories for me,
I have not met anyone with them till date, never
talked to them. Only chat on hangouts.

He threw my laptop on the couch and got up and
came to me - tell me the truth, Kamini, with whom
have you been celebrating with me? If I did not tell
the truth, then I will make you feel that you will
remember your whole life.

I vowed a lot, cried a lot, begged, but the lamp had
no effect.

By leaving just one laptop open, all my family
members, my honour, my honour and dignity were
at stake.

There was no conversation between us for two
days, I tried hard, repeatedly apologized to Deepak,
repeatedly explained to him, repeatedly begged -
all stories are lies, are fictional, none are true.

But the problem was that all the stories were written about an incident that had really happened in our lives. So due to this Deepak was convinced that in his absence, I have kept wrong relations with others The next day, when Deepak returned home in the evening, he started drinking whiskey, turned on the AC of the bedroom, switched one of the two phones. After a while, the house bell rang. He got up on his own.

When he returned, he had a 24-25-year-old girl with him. Wearing a white T-shirt and jeans, nicely stuffed body, fair-skinned and very beautiful girl. I was looking at the lamp with questions.

Deepak asked the girl to sit on the sofa near him, regardless of me. When she sat down, Deepak made a peg and gave it to her. Both cheered and started drinking.

I thought with gusto, maybe this girl is a girl. Means Deepak too wants to take revenge on me by fucking it on my bed in my house.
I did not say anything, I thought if this would calm their anger, then I will bear it too.

They kept talking to each other, both of them kept laughing and I sat like an idiot watching them both drinking alcohol.

After drinking two pegs, Deepak got up and came
to me, holding me with his arm and standing. I
thought that maybe now they will get me out of the
bedroom. But Deepak caught my sari and started
pulling it open.

I protested against this - Deepak, what are you
doing?
But he was just as obsessed.

That girl also said - Let it be sir, let them go, or I will
go.
But Deepak scolded him too.

My saree opened, then I grabbed my blouse, I
wanted to stop, and in a blink of an eye, Rubia's
blouse burst in a single stroke.
After that Deepak pulled my bra too and broke her
strap and separated from my body and then forcibly
tore my petticoat and separated from my body.
Within a minute I was completely naked.

Deepak pushed me mercilessly and dropped me on
the bed and then took off his clothes, he too
became completely naked.
Then said to that girl - Sheena, come here.
When that girl got up from the sofa, Deepak said -
Take off all your clothes.

She said, Sir, if there is any problem in both of you,
then I leave, let me stay.

Deepak also scolded him and said - You have been given me money or not, for what. Do not get caught in our affair, do what I say.

The poor girl too removed her clothes with great care. A beautiful young body.

Deepak laid me on the bed and climbed on my chest and sat down, his taut cock was near my face.
But Deepak said to Sheena - Sheena sucked my life, my cock.

Now that poor doll of money, where did he have to refuse. She came down to me and started sucking my husband's cock in her mouth in front of my face. After a little kiss Deepak said - Just sucked a lot, come on up.

The girl started thinking that there was already a woman lying on the bed, where did she come upstairs.
So Deepak got up and grabbed her hand and offered her on the bed and then brought the girl over to me.

A continuous stream of tears was flowing from my eyes.

When that girl lay down on me, Deepak offered a condom on his cock, placed it on Sheena's puddle

and started fucking her. I felt so ashamed of myself
that my husband is lying on my own and fucking
me, how big punishment my husband has given
me. The husband who loved me very much.

Well, when Deepak had finished fucking Sheena,
he told Sheena - Look darling, now you get my
goods off my hand. But my goods should fall on the
face of this dishonour.

The girl began to turn on Deepak and then after
some time Deepak's cock hit the hot semen. The
semen that I was very happy to have on my body,
the semen that I used to lick and drink.

But today that semen seemed to me like poison or
like an acid.
My whole mouth was filled with Deepak's semen.
people even without his knowledge.

While Deepak and I once had sex with someone
else in front of each other in a swinger club, but he
was in front of her, he was aware.

But after reading my stories Deepak felt as if I am a
thirsty of some cock, a very sensual woman. I am a
cheeky, a whore, a prostitute who needs cocks all
the time.

I should talk to Deepak again before going to sleep at night, but he said - tomorrow I will give you the biggest problem of your life.
I started crying again, apologizing to him.
But Deepak kicked me out of my bedroom.

I also went and lay down in the second bedroom, and started wondering what Deepak would do to me tomorrow. Don't just divorce me. I am afraid I do not know when I fell asleep.

After the work was over, the girl left. Deepak slept on the same bed naked.

I got up and came to the bathroom and cried a lot, cried out loud, and wept as soon as I cried. Today I had to face unlimited insult.

But after that day Deepak's anger like that slowly started to cool down. Slowly we both started getting back to normal, and after about two and a half months our life became absolutely normal.

I talked to Deepak and explained the whole thing to him, he also understood that I had only told someone about my mind, but did not have sex with anyone without knowing of Deepak. It took time but Deepak understood my state of mind by repeatedly explaining to me.

Some more time passed, and after about two and a half months, Deepak and I had sex. Of course, while having sex, I remembered that day and I cried again.

After that day, Deepak's anger started to cool down slowly. Slowly we both started getting back to normal, and after about two and a half months our life became absolutely normal. I talked to Deepak and explained the whole thing to him, he also understood that I had only told someone about my mind, but did not have sex with anyone without knowing of Deepak. It took time but Deepak understood my state of mind by repeatedly explaining to me.

Some more time passed, and after about two and a half months, Deepak and I had sex. Of course, while having sex, I remembered that day and I cried again.

But Deepak told me - Look, Preeti, if any feeling comes to your heart for anyone, then tell me, I will try my best to fulfil every desire of your heart.
But I still thought it appropriate to keep the feelings of my mind in mind.

About 6 months had passed, then came our wedding anniversary.
I asked Deepak - what gift will I give this time on marriage?

Deepak said- I am thinking of a surprise gift.
I thought someone will give a jewel or saree. By the
way, we were also thinking of getting a new car, I
thought that maybe it will take a new car, it had
more chances.

Deepak said - Sal Girah's party will only do both of
us, and outside in a hotel.
I was also happy.

On the day of the wedding year, I was very happy
since morning. Go to the beauty parlour to have full
waxing of your body, get bikini wax done, and get
your smoothie too smooth. Dressed up like a full
bride and got ready in the evening and waited for
Deepak's arrival.

In the evening, he came and after a while, we both
walked towards the hotel.

We both went to our room after going to the hotel.
First came the alcohol. Sometimes I give company
to Deepak, so Deepak made a small peg for me.
After putting a little peg in each mood, we both
went downstairs to eat in the dining hall.

Had food, then we strolled around the swimming
pool in the hotel garden, talking to the romantic.
Seeing the opportunity in between, Deepak also
kissed me, suppressed my mother. Now it was a

romantic day, so I did not stop Deepak at all but enjoyed his romance.

Then we increased the status of love and then Deepak said - let's go to the room, let's do something. Now you are not filled with a heart to see. Now I want to drink a drink of these juicy lips.

When we both came back to our room, Deepak dropped me on the bed as soon as I came. Tucked the fingers of my hands in my fingers, pulled my hands over my head and started sucking my lips with my lips.

I was also in full mood, completely warm, ready to give. I was also showing full heat, sucking the lamp. My husband is sucking me for the last 4 years, so what would I be ashamed of today?
My lips sucked, my cheeks were cut off from my teeth by eating a lamp, licking my tongue and making my whole face wet. Lick kisses on my neck and earbud make me very tickled, Deepak knew this, so he kissed me a lot around my neck and temple, torturing me a lot.
I was going crazy by laughing at the tickle caused by his touch.

Then Deepak woke up immediately - Madarchod naked me!
He said.

He often abuses me during sex, I like to eat
abuses, so I woke up smiling and I opened all the
clothes of the lamp with my hands. When his tights
were removed, his taut cocks appeared in front of
me.
I caught hold of it, but when I started sucking his
cock, he said - don't stop now.
When I got up and stood up, she opened my sari
herself, took off my blouse, opened my bra,
removed my petticoat and panty too, asked me to
bare the bed and sit on the bed.

I went to bed and lay down and looked at Deepak
when he came and lay down on me, did something
himself, or asked me to do something.
But nothing like this happened.

Then the room bell rang. I was very surprised that
who has come this time to stall our love.

I would say something, even before Deepak went
and opened the door, an English boy came inside.
I quickly covered my naked body with a bedsheet.
I asked Deepak - Deepak, who is this, and why did
you call it inside?
Deepak said- My love… this is a surprise gift for
you.
I asked - Surprise gift?
He said- Yes, I felt very bad that day, which I did
with you. Then I thought, even earlier I shared my
will with you. You have sex with someone else in

front of me, I have sex with someone else. So, if you have had sex with anyone without my knowledge then what is the wrong thing. But on that day, I did not like it too, by lying on top of it. So today I have brought this gift to you. You can have sex with it on your own today. If you want, you can also take revenge by burning me. I wouldn't mind

I said- Deepak, I don't want to take any revenge from you. Yes, there is no doubt that I liked your gift. The rest, if it's a weapon is also good, I will be happy to make a connection with it, but I want both of us to enjoy this gift together.
Deepak agreed.

That English boy's name was Jordan but we were calling him Jordi. Now when everything became clear, Jordi also took off his clothes. Milk-like fair complexion, 6 feet in height, broad shoulders. Going to the gym has also made me a good body. And when he took off his trunks, it was found that he was a very good man, about 9 inches long and thick cocks, milk-like blond cocks, ruddy red colour. The jaunt was completely cleaned. Shaved hair also.

I told Deepak - Deepak I really liked your gift.
Deepak said - So see what you are doing, have fun with your gift.

I felt a little ashamed, but I had done this before, so I removed the sheet wrapped on my body and came down from the bed completely naked like the idol of Khajuraho. I went and sat in front of Jordi and caught his blonde cock in my hand.

It was quite strong and tough. I took his cock straight in my mouth. One thing is common among all kinds of men in the world, everyone has the same taste of cocks. Slightly salty.
I sucked his ruddy red top like children suck lollipops. Well, the fact is right, in childhood, lollipop and youth like to enjoy sucking both cocks equally. While I was sucking Jordi's cocks, Deepak also came near me and stood up.

I caught Deepak's cocks on the other hand. One hand 9 inch milk-like blonde British cocks, in the other hand 6-inch black Indian cocks. Of course both of them were bitter, but if the new thing tastes more, then I was sucking more of Jordi's cock.

Then my husband said to Jordi - Jordi, I want you to fuck my wife so much today, fuck me so much that I do not want to fuck her for a month.
Jordi said- ok sir.
And Jordi raised me on his lap, laying on the bed.

I also opened my thighs for her.

Jordi sat down and kissed my maiden, then licked.
A professional man is a professional. The
brother-in-law had a big way of licking. The
brother-in-law tortured me a lot.

When my girl started dropping water due to licking,
I called Deepak to myself and I took Deepak's cock
in my mouth. Really enjoyed it. On one side I was
licking and I was sucking a cock on the other side.

Then Jordi got up and put his head of cock on my
head. I looked up at Jordi and, looking into my
eyes, he removed his top in my shirt.
Now the 9-inch Aloda will penetrate the 6-inch
Alududdi, once with difficulty. 'Ummh… ahh…
hah… yah…' came out of my mouth lightly.
Jordi asked- what happened?
I said - is fat.
He laughed and said - Tall too, just to see.

And his point was also correct, as he licked his
cock in my puddle, my eyes kept coming out. Such
a thick and long cock. Within two minutes I knew
that this long racehorse, like a lamp, would not
come over me in 5-7 minutes. My pleasure was on
the seventh sky with bigger and better cocks. I was
just doing my stretches, lying down under him.
Deepak was also standing near me, but now I did
not pay any attention to him, I was just having my
own fun. Deepak turned Jordi's face towards him

and put his cock in his mouth. Jordi was fucking me
and sucking my husband's cock.

I asked Jordi - do you do this too?
He said - Ma'am, I give all kinds of service. If you
want, you can also kill my ass, and if you want, I
can kill their ass too.
I laughed and asked Deepak - why is Deepak
thinking, if he complains of constipation, the doctor
is with him.

All three of us laughed after listening to me, but
Deepak flatly denied this.

I fell for the first time in 10 minutes with Jordi's
fantastic fuck. My water splashed white water on
the edge several times. But right now my heart was
not filled with sex.
I patted Jordi and said- Well done Jordi, just keep
pouring my water again and again, till you can
remove it.
Jordi said- I can fuck you all night without stopping.

Deepak asked- Where are you from when you bring
so much stamina?
Jordi said- I have a doctor friend, he gives me
some special medicines, from which my cock also
grew and I also get unprecedented sex power.
Deepak asked quickly - oh man, wow, then tell me
about that doctor too?
Jordi said - no, he only treats professionals.

I said - Jordi, wait a little… I started hurting with
legs raised, I become a mare, then fuck from
behind.

Jordi took his cock out of my cock, I became a
mare on the bed.
Seeing the shape of my cool round ass, Jordi said-
I would like to get your ass killed?
By the way, I had already killed 2-3 people, but I did
not have the courage to take this thick pestle in my
ass, so I refused - oh no Jordi, I take your huge
cock in my ass. Does not want to be annihilated.
You just keep enjoying me in my mouth.

My husband was also standing with me holding his
cock in my hand but neither I was sucking his cock,
nor was playing with his cock. Their cocks had
become loose due to no action. They were shaking
their cocks just after seeing me fucking with that
Englishman. But maybe he was not enjoying it
either.

Then he sat on the bed near us and started making
videos of my fuck on his mobile.

After 15 minutes, my second water fell. Now I was
tired of my fuck going on for the last half hour, so I
asked Jordi to take some rest while I needed rest
Was feeling
He was still standing that way.

My husband made one drink each. This time I too pulled the entire peg. Whiskey also showed its effect right away, I was only watching Jordi in the drunken Ghumar. Of course, he was drinking the peg sitting on the sofa, but his cock was full taut with his stomach.

I told Jordi - can you roll your cock in my glass? After listening to me, Jordi smiled and got up and came to me, he put his cock in my glass and then he drenched me with alcohol.
In reality, the taste and taste of this wine were different.

Then Deepak said- Why shouldn't Preeti drink liquor drip from your body?

Standing at the table, I was given a glass of wine in my hand. I slowly dropped that glass on my body, cold ice with alcohol, dripping from my breasts, both Deepak and Jordi licked the liquor from my mummies and as the liquor flowed down from my body, it passed down from my momma to my The stomach, licking my clit and thighs, went to my feet.

After getting licked by two men, my girls started getting wet again. This experience was very erotic. I started to take cocks again. When the peg was over, Deepak and Jordi again sat on the sofa and they made another peg and started drinking.

I came down from the table and went and sat
directly on Jordi's lap, grabbed his cock and sat
down on my chair. I and Jordi were looking into
each other's eyes and I swallowed Jordi's whole
cock with my whimper.
Jordi said - is your pussy very thirsty?
I said- Yes, when the dish is pleasing, even after
filling the stomach, it does not fill the intention.

I put both my hands on Jordi's shoulder and started
slowly getting myself down. Jordi's cool cock
reaches my stomach.

Deepak said - Why my life, today it seems that you
will quench your thirst with all your strength.
I did not like Deepak to speak in this beautiful
moment of pleasure, so I said with pity -
Motherfucker.

When Deepak stepped back, Jordi picked me up in
his arms in the same condition and then went and
lay down on the bed. Now I had an open space, so
I jumped on top of Jordi's cock. Bounced until I was
tired, my breath did not swell.

When I got tired, Jordi came down on his own,
laying me down. I wrapped my legs around his
waist - kill me Jordi, fuck me so much… fuck me so
that my thirst for births can be quenched.
Now Jordi was such a brilliant man, that his doctor
friend was giving him medicines, it was amazing.

The hard cocks of Jordi went all the way inside my puddle and erased all my itching.

When I showered for the third time, Jordi also fell. But even after the loss, his cock was very hard, it was probably the effect of his medicine.

I calmed down and lay down cold. Then maybe I fell asleep.

Around 3 in the morning I felt like someone was doing something to me. When I opened my eyes, Jordi was fucking me.
I asked - what happened?
He said - Your husband has said, once I fuck you and fuck.

I looked at Deepak, he was getting drunk. What was my objection, even after midnight, I was like this man. But this time Jordi fucking me very strongly. Made the whole train mine.

Now my girl was also hurting, and was not taking the name of loss, nor was giving up water, the dry skin was peeled off by the hard cock of Jordi. Now I was feeling that because of this dry fuck all my itchiness of my pudding would be relaxed. After about a quarter of an hour, my water fell down with difficulty, only a little, I fell right.

But this fuck made me so tired that when I returned
to the bathroom after mooting, I was unable to walk
and fell down on the floor. She lay down there and
did not know when she slept. I do not know when I
picked up the lamp in the morning and brought it
back home.

After three o'clock in the afternoon, my eyes
opened, and I looked at my own house. I got up
and went to the bathroom. Saline urine also came
as if it was acid, it burnt from the egg. I also had
difficulty walking due to the pain of the puddle.

Going to the kitchen, made some tea, and ate
bread together because I was feeling very hungry.

Deepak was still sleeping. I drank tea and wrapped
it with a lamp again. I kissed Deepak while
sleeping, he said in his sleep - what happened?
I said - nothing, just to say thank you.

My friend gave me pain on my birthday

My dear friends, how are you all!
My name is Suhani Chaudhary and I am 22 years old, I study only in Delhi. Actually, I am from Saharanpur district of Uttar Pradesh but now I live in a hostel in Delhi with my friend Tanvi.

Since childhood, I am one of the few lucky humans who have probably never failed in mathematics, never been caught doing anything wrong, there are no light spots on the face and the colour is blond and absolutely smooth and the face is very cheerful. Youth has a different shine on it. The body is of the perfect height.

Many people keep asking my figure, so for their information, tell me that my figure was normal before but now it has become 36-26-36. I have looked very beautiful and innocent since childhood, and even till last year. Some of my friends even used to say that everyone has grown up, but Suhani has grown bigger than just the body, but even with the appearance, she still looks innocent like children.

My nature is also very soft and I talk most lovingly, no attitude, no tantrums, but when someone starts bothering me more and more, I just stop talking.

I have a boyfriend named Karan but he lives in another city. To know more about me, new readers are requested to read my previous stories as well and if you like it, then also like it, I feel very good about it.
So let's move on to the next story.

It had been more than a week since Harshil had come here and I and Tanvi were busy with their college life. The pressure of studies had increased significantly and attention was distracted from studying here and there.
Next month my birthday was going to come, so Tanvi asked- What is the plan on his birthday this time, where is the party going?
I said, man, what kind of party you have to study, otherwise this time I will fail. Birthdays come every year, we will celebrate again sometime.

Most of my time was spent talking on the phone with Karan, we were always on either the phone or chat. The readers who wrote my previous story Honeymoon celebrated in brother's wedding Did not read, let me tell them a little bit about Karan.

I and Karan met at my maternal uncle's wedding, Karan was on behalf of the girl and used to do jobs. She is very cute and handsome in appearance. I also look very cute and innocent, so Tanvi used to call us both as cute couples. Since then, we both started loving each other.

Now love cannot be said whether it was true or not… but we both loved talking to each other, we used to share almost everything. I did not tell him about Harshil, otherwise, his heart would have broken.

He was going to come to Delhi for my birthday. I had met him only once in marriage till now, and he had done all that in between.

Slowly the time passed and the next month also came, my birthday was only two days later, Karan had also come to Delhi and was staying with some of his relatives. When I received her call, she told-
Baby, I have come to Delhi, let's meet tomorrow.
I told him to suffer like this - No Babu, not now, the papers are coming, we will meet you the day after tomorrow.
He said- Please man… I have come from so far just for you, let's meet tomorrow.

I said- No man, please understand, if you come out of the hostel tomorrow, you will not be allowed the day after tomorrow, the warden of the hostel does

not go out every day, this time I want to celebrate
my birthday with you.
Karan said- Okay okay, can you come outside the
hostel gate for 10 minutes?
I said yes, she can.

The next day in the evening, Karan got a call and
Tanvi and I went outside the hostel to meet him.
Karan brought his relative's car and was waiting a
little distance from the main gate. After about 2
months we were seeing each other face to face.

After looking at her, I ran away and hugged her
hard. We hugged like this for 30-40 seconds.
Tanvi said - I am also Karan, I and Suhani have
come along, you may have forgotten me?
I smiled at Sharma and started looking down.

Karan too smiled and said- Tanvi ji, you have a
very big hand in joining us.
Then Karan and Tanvi also hugged and we started
talking about standing here and there.

We did not know when it was half an hour while
talking, the sun was starting to fall and it was seen
drowning in distant clouds.
Tanvi said - "Let's go now, otherwise the warden
will not let me go anywhere tomorrow."

I did not want to go away from Karan but there was
no other option, I told Karan - I have to go.

Karan said- no one, see you tomorrow, take care of yourself.

I hugged Karan out loud and then broke away and said - Let's go.

Karan said- Just a hug? Give me a goodbye

I immediately remembered the wedding night, I said - absolutely not, this trick will not go here.

Tanvi also started laughing and said- It is still evening, Karanji, there is a lot of time in the 3-4 hours of the night.

He started smiling and said- Okay, I will stop here till 3 o'clock then.

I understood what Karan would not go without. I came very fast to Karan and held his head close to his ear with his two hands and put my lips on his lips and kissed loudly and both of us stood with the help of the car.

Karan did not expect this, perhaps… then his eyes were opened with surprise. Then slowly we both started doing a deep and long kiss. Tanvi was watching, tearing her eyes silently, she must be thinking how shameless I am becoming.

After about a minute, she said - if I say open the car seat, do the program ahead here too.

When we came back in our mood, we separated and I started walking in Harabada's turn and by bolt and came to the hostel.

Tanvi also returned in a while.

I told Tanvi - You are not ashamed, someone is enjoying their romantic moments and every time you interrupt the whole fun by speaking in between. Tanvi said - Good sir… If there is such a fire, then tomorrow, a lot of sex left, by the way, the birthday party is an excuse, in fact, it has to fuck you, right? I laughed and said- Don't improve, always think the same thing.
Then we had dinner and slept.

Karan got a call at exactly 12 o'clock in the night and he said - Dear Suhani Chaudhary on Happy Birthday.
I bid - thank you very much.
Then Karan said - how was the gift?
I bid - which gift?
He said - Get out of the sheet and look at the table on the side.
I saw that there was a gift box there, I said - Hey !!, thank you, dear, I understood that she had got this gift placed by Tanvi.

Tanvi was also up and she too wished me a happy birthday.
Karan said on the phone - look at the gift open!
So I opened, there was a very beautiful red coloured saree inside it. Then Tanvi placed a box in my hand and said - This is a gift from my side.

When I opened it, she had a matching coloured blouse and petticoat for me.

I said both thanks. Then Karan said - If you come wearing this tomorrow, I will feel good, I want to see you tomorrow as my wife.
I said- Hey, how will I come wearing this, yet the fitting of the blouse would not have been done.
So Tanvi said- Don't worry about it, I had made all the fittings according to your size. Karan had already told me that I should buy all this according to this saree.

I was happy and said- you both had already made a good gift plan.
Karan said on the phone - yes dear, now you can sleep if you want, see you tomorrow for the party.
I said - okay sir! And I like the gift very much for both of you.

Probably the first time someone gifted me a sari. Then I slept smiling, keeping everything the same.

The next day we both woke up comfortably, Tanvi woke up and once again told me a happy birthday. My hostel friends also told me Happy Birthday and some boys from the hostel also sent gifts to the guards… Know if someone is a college girl, then it makes so much for her.

Most of the people had gone to college to do classes… but Tanvi and I had taken a break.
Later in the afternoon, Tanvi and I called the cab and went out of the hostel in simple clothes and took party clothes for the party.

On the way, both of us stopped at the parlour and changed clothes. For the first time, I wore the saree at the farewell party of the school itself, that too was the mother.
I went to the bathroom wearing a sexy red-coloured push-up bra and panties and then came out wearing a blouse and petticoat, Tanvi also took a blouse that tied to the string instead of the back hook.

Tanvi helped me out when I came out.
Tanvi said, "Suhani, your clothes are checked on you, see that the fitting has come right." Looking very beautiful, today Karan's heart will fall out of your feet.
I said smiling lightly on her shoulder and said -
Come on, she speaks anything crazy. Now walk out!
And we both reached the parlour, Wali.

She also put a little sexy make-up on our big cutie.
We gave them money and sat in the cab to go to the birthday party.

The cab driver was also looking at me in the mirror repeatedly, so Tanvi said - Brother, look at the road!
So, looking at the panic on the road, he started driving.

We both reached Karan's address and got down from the car and gave the cab money and went into the house. Karan was waiting for us, as soon as he saw me his mouth was open, tearing eyes and staring at me. It was lovely to see her so seductively like children.

Tanvi broke the silence and said - will someone say something or will everyone keep watching like this? Then both of us started laughing, Karan welcomed us, we hugged and came and sat on the sofa.

Karan was sitting in front and his eyes were coming back and stopping at me.
I said - what happened, I am not looking good in these clothes?
So said, friend Suhani, you are looking so beautiful in this saree that my eyes are not moving away from you, it looks like an angel has come down.
Red colour looks very cute and sexy on you.

I bid - Your gift is very beautiful, thank you.
Karan said - has become more beautiful after you wear it.
I started looking under Sharma.

Tanvi said- I will not mind if someone compliments me.
On this, Karan started laughing and said- Yes Tanvi Ji, you are looking very beautiful too.
Karan asked- just both of you have come to the party?
I said - we are just both, will not feed anything?

So Karan brought cold drinks and snacks from the kitchen and placed them on the table.
To tease Karan, I deliberately raised my glass by leaning forward more than smiling, the sari's pallu fell down and my boobs started showing from the big neck of the blouse.

Karan was absolutely shocked and I saw the movement in his pants, then he sat across his leg and I started laughing.

Tanvi was also seeing all this and looked down and smiled. Tanvi said- Let's cut the cake.
Karan went and brought the cake from the fridge and placed it on the table. Tanvi lit a candle with it. Then we cut the cake and fed each other wholeheartedly.

Karan said - Suhani, the cake is left on your lips.
I tried to clean, it didn't happen.
Karan said- Bring, I remove.

And came to me and kissed my lips with his lips,
licked and ate the cake.

I was not expecting her to do such a thing, then my
eyes opened with surprise. Seeing the warmth of
Tanvi's case, bid - Let's eat food, then I have to go
to a hostel or else the warden will come to know.
Suhani, you come tomorrow, I will handle
everything.
I was happy how intelligent Tanvi is in these
matters.

I and Karan got Tanvi dinner but since I was not
hungry yet, Karan and I did not eat, just ate a light
meal. After eating food, Tanvi called the cab. It was
night, and Karan went to leave him in the car and
said thank you, man.
Tanvi said- You considered your birthday well,
come live tomorrow!
And whisper said in my ear - fucked well, and if you
want to get ass to Leo, Karan will definitely be
happy.

I said while hitting him on the shoulder - you are
absolutely shameless, come on… I will see what to
do.

We came to bye-bye bol and went to Tanvi Hostel.

I and Karan came in and locked the doors.
I bid - where are your relatives?

So he said- those people have gone to Agra for the home of an uncle, they will come by tomorrow evening.

Karan went and put on romantic music and came to me, sat on his knees and extended his right hand towards me and asked - Suhani Chaudhary, will you dance with me?
I smiled and gave my hand to him and we started dancing slowly.

He took his one hand on my white velvet back and started to dance by holding my hand with the other hand. After dancing like this for a while, I put my head on his chest and filled him in the arms and we kept moving while dancing slowly.

Karan picked me up in the dock and took me to his room. He took me to the room and laid me on the bed and sat next to me himself.

Karan was so romantic that he laid flowers on the bed. Now there was no doubt about what was going to happen next.
I said - you are fully prepared for the second honeymoon.
Karan said - anything for you dear!

I started smiling and got up and sat down on my knees. I said - is there any hurry today or like that day?

Karan said- No Babu, no one is going to disturb us today, we can love comfort.
I said- Hmm… I will be in the bathroom once.
He said- Okay.

Now I got up and came to the bathroom and started fixing myself in front of the mirror by doing the bathroom, correcting the hair again, applying red lipstick, setting the saree and setting the blouse down so that the bulbs started appearing more. Then I entered the bedroom inside.

Karan was waiting for me while looking at the bathroom door. He notices me and says - today you will kill me.
When I stood up near her, she immediately laid her hand on my waist while sitting.

I lifted her face up in my hands and placed my lips on her lips and started kissing with love. Initially, we were kissing with love, but it was making me very excited to move my waist and stomach. Now our love was not filled with lust, I was sucking her lips, sometimes she was coming back to my lips, even to our tongue in each other's mouth and Umm… Umm… in the room. Umm… umm… was getting intoxicating voices.

After some time, when I turned away, the pallu of my saree slipped and fell and I was standing in

front of her in a blouse and bottom saree with blond
coarse boobs and in the middle was my waist.
I said - will you keep watching or will you do
something?

Karan came to me and went back and opened the
blouse cords and removed the front. Now in front of
her, there were boobs stuck in my red bra which
were falling down due to their weight and my
breathing.
Karan's eyes were torn to see such a form of
mine… He said, man, you look like an innocent girl
who does not know anything about all these
things… but in reality, there is quite a devil.
unbelievable. You know that my friends were
looking at you at the wedding on that day, saying
that it will not go away from you, just looks decent,
it will not talk about shame.

I said - now Sharif girls also have erotic feelings
baby… and that image is meant to show the world,
and now what shame on you!
He said - yes it is, now what shame between each
other.

I was in full mood to fuck, so I said - what is the
mood to talk today?
So he said- No man, it is not so.
I said - if it is not, then hold it!
And after lifting it from the ground, gave the sari's
pallu in her hand and said- Don't know what to do?

He said - what to do? You only tell me.
I said- what Duryodhana did with Draupadi… Just my sari will be finished in a while.

Karan was happy and started pulling my saree and I started moving around and my sari completely fell apart.
I said - it takes a lot of experience to take off the sari?
So he started laughing.

I said - will you see magic?
And opened the pulse of his petticoat and dropped it down too. Now I was just standing in my sexy red bra and panty and the open hair falling on my half face was flying lightly and it was in full clothes. Although his dick was tanned in his pants.

Seeing me in this condition, he immediately came to me and hugged me. Her dick was rubbing on my pussy from outside, so I got more excited. I took off his T-shirt and threw out the vest.

Karan shoved his lower pyjamas down and turned from side to side. His cock was completely tanned in his tail.
I said - why are you drowning your cock, take off the briefs too.
He said - Come on, let's take each other off.

She slid down on the side of my panty with a finger
and I pulled her briefs down. Then he did not take
any time to remove my bra and both of us stood
naked in front of each other.

For a while, he kept looking at my naked body and I
at him.
I bid - will you keep on looking or do you intend to
do something?
Karan started smiling and said- Janu… lying in front
of us all night, we will rest easy.

He came up to me and rubbed my boobs with love
in his hands as if the dough was kneading, my
sobbing voice started to come out and I started
sighing, sighing. I also stuffed her neck in my arms
and started kissing with love. While doing this, we
came and fell on the bed while walking and he
came over me kissing me with lust and rubbing my
boobs.

Then Karan started to kiss my left boob full of lips
and started sucking the nipple. I was closing the
eyes with my teeth and pressing the lips. Karan
was slowly going down and kissed on the stomach.
My stomach was fluttering due to sexuality and
passion and I was breathing fast… breathless…
even though I was feeling a little tickle, even smiling
and moving up and down on the bed.

Now, Karan came directly to my pussy and was very full and started eating. I immediately opened my mouth and cried out loud and got up and sat down with my hands raised.
Karan was licking my pussy, the touch of his wet tongue was making me very happy.

Then he started to put his tongue in and out of my pussy and I went on filling it with pleasure and lust. I pressed her head on my pussy with one hand and her legs were being crossed and pressed into her pussy. I loudly say Ummah… Ahh… Hah… Yah…. sobbing sounds were being taken.

In a short time, my pussy was smooth and due to the smoothness, it started glowing to the outside. I opened my legs and told Karan - now you sit!
So he hung up on the bed and lay down.

I filled his dick in my soft hands and lovingly did it from top to bottom so that the skin of his dick was behind and the mouth of the dick came out. Karan said, looking at me - Ahhh… Suhani… how soft are your hands… long long fingers, long long nails, red nail polish on them, God has made every part of you sexy.
I gave him a smile while looking at him and kissed one of his cock's mouth and touched it with his tongue on the hole of the cock, and he burst and Karan gave a loud sigh….

Perhaps boys like to kiss them with their mouths.

So I started sucking her dick down all over the mouth and playing with the tongue touching the dick. Karan's body was fully tanned and had grown to about seven inches. He was fat, so I removed the cocks out of my mouth and sat next to him and started caressing with his hand.

Karan said - What happened, Janu, it was so much fun, why did you stop.
I said - so that you do not leave and my fun is not complete.
Karan said - Okay, let's start. You lay on the bed.

I lay down on my bed, and Karan came between my legs.
I said - why are you torturing now? Do not pour…
My pussy has been yearning for your cock since. It is time to control myself, just not now.
Karan smiled and said - okay honey, here you are.

Karan spread both my legs and lifted me towards the bed and put his dick on my fluttering pussy and said - sir?
I said please don't put it.
Because it was time for me to fuck, then I said - pour slowly, it has been a long time, so maybe there is pain.
Karan put less than half of the cock in my pussy, then my sigh came out due to pain and pleasure.

Karan looked and said - what happened, should I
stop?
I said no-no… you keep on.
Now Karan slowly started pushing the cock inside
and his cock began to go in, making it a forceful
place in the walls of my pussy.

He did not immediately but was slowly poured out
of love, so I continued to have the sweet pain of
putting him until he was completely gone. And as
soon as I got inside, dick touched my G-spot and
touched it and got stuck.
Ahhhhhhhhhhh… I took a loud sigh.

Karan understood that he was pushing his cock a
little bit inside, and I was taking slow light CEEE…
CEEE… sobbing voice due to friction.

After doing a few moments like this, I said - now
you can start fucking.
Karan said - Dude, I enjoyed it very slowly! As your
pussy was going to hold on to my cock and was
pressing, the fun came. Come on, I start fucking
slowly today.
I nodded yes

Karan took out the cock and slowly re-inserted it
and pulled it out, then pulled it out again and
started doing… ah… ah… ahhhh….

His cock was going in like a train and when I got stuck outside the pussy, I would get shocked and my sight would come out. I was looking up into her eyes and shaking my head in yes and in my eyes I was saying - keep on fucking, please.

Then slowly his speed also increased and the light sound of Patta Patta started to hit our body. I had also stepped up the vigil and was loudly sighing… uh… ahh… ahhh….
Karan was also doing a lot of hmmm… hmm… hmm….

I was moving up and down on the bed, watching him and leaning over me, I was going to fuck. After stopping for about 7-8 minutes like this, he stopped due to breathlessness and lay next to me on the bed and started panting.

I was panting too fast… Ummm… Ahhh… and seeing Karan moving my boobs up and down.
I did - enjoyed it, man… do it next!
So he said - I am going to breathe, otherwise I will die on you.
I started smiling and said- Oh no… I will let you die like this.
I bid - I keep you lying down.

I rubbed her cock and then started sucking her mouth lightly while lying on the bed Karan was doing hmm… hmm… hmm….

When her body was full again, I came on top of her and sat down on her knees, my open hair came hanging next to Karan's face and I looked in her eyes and said, ready?
When Karan nodded yes, I gave my hand down and rested his dick on my pussy and slowly took it back in the pussy and filled it a little.

Now I started to take it back and forth with Karan in a lusty pussy and Karan was loving my boobs. I was lying on her, uh… ummah… ahhh… ahh… yah… aaa… hah… ahhhh….

Karan was also looking into my eyes moving up and down on the bed. In between, I was doing whatever on her lips.

Then after about 4-5 minutes I got tired and lay down on it. My boobs were adjoining his chest and his cock was still lying in the pussy and I and he were breathing loudly… ahhhh….

Karan said- Are you tired, Babu?
So I said - you can be tired, I can be tired too.
He said - Let's get some rest!
So I started resting lying on her.

Then I got up and stood and started drinking water from the bottle placed on the dressing table on the side.

I walked up to Karan and gave him water too. He also drank water from the bottle and returned it to me.

As soon as I came back to bed, he said - Wait, stop there!
And he came after me and said- Put one foot on the bed, stand and lean forward slightly.
So I bowed down like that.

Karan came from behind on my pussy and started rubbing his dick on my pussy, then I started to feel like a big batch.
I bid - do not pour, what are you rubbing?
So Karan entered the ground with a gag and I shook the front with a slight ouch.

Now, Karan grabbed my waist with hands, then started banging me. I ah… ah… ummah… ahh… hah… yah… ahhh… doing loud noises and my booby, hairy body was shaking back and forth from her bumps.

Karan too hmm… hmm… hmm… was going to Chode and the voice of Patta Patta was coming.

By now, Karan had increased his speed a lot and was continuously going for 8–9 minutes. When I was getting close to losing, I started saying very loudly 'Ahhh ... Ahhh ... Baby and fast ... and fast ...'

Karan threw all his strength and started fucking faster, by doing this he also got closer to the loss.

After a while, my legs started twitching, so I put my hands on my back and stopped Karan, and after falling apart, she fell on her legs and thighs and vomited on the bed.
Karan was close to losing at that time, then immediately came to my pussy with the last shaking from the back, ummah… ummah… meh… started fucking and while leaving his 3-4 pitches, ahhh… and I got a pussy in my pussy. He came and lay down and started panting.

I was vomiting and looking at him, I was laughing. Her dick was stained in her own semen and my pussy water, and water and dripping drops of her semen were dripping from my pussy which she had put in her pussy.

Keeping the elbow in the bed, I turned my head towards his head and asked him - Enjoyed, right? He rolled his hand in my hanging hair and said - Enjoyed it dear Janu, Happy Birthday once again.

I smiled and kissed her lips and put one of her legs on her legs and lay down fast and we both started slowing down.

For about half an hour, we kept clinging to each other in such a naked state, I had my head placed

on his chest, with my ears fixed and we kept on
talking here and there. Then I got up and went to
the bathroom and cleaned myself.
Then came back to the room and started wearing
clothes.

So he said - just once? Don't wear it please man,
will fuck you once more.
I said - are you still not full of heart?
Karan said - The boy whose heart fills you will be
the biggest pussy of the world.
I said - Oh Baba, don't wear it!
And put their scattered clothes in the room and put
them on the side.

By now, both of us were hungry, so we came to
dinner. Now, because there was no one in the
house except the two of us, we were roaming
around the whole house. We had dinner and kept
talking here and there. Then I and Karan together
cleaned the utensils. In between, we used to tease
each other's hands with each other, sometimes I
used to rub her cock, sometimes she would rub my
ass and both of us would laugh.

It had been 2-3 hours of fucking us. I said - let's go
to sleep now.
Karan said- Dude, after so much time I have met
you today and I will not let you sleep at all.
I jokingly said - what will you do if you do not sleep?

Karan said - Today I will love with all my heart, I will love it completely… I do not know when I should meet again.
I said - Good Babu, please do love, today whatever you ask, I will not refuse, sure promise.

Karan became happy and said- Think, don't refuse later?
I said - I will not, my friend.
He said - Okay, let's go to the bedroom again!

And we come to the bedroom.

I sat on the bed and sat at the door and started watching me with great love. And why do you see… the queen of her dreams was sitting on her bed in front of her without crossing her legs without clothes.
I asked - what happened, are you watching like this?
Karan said - I see, sometimes God is so kind to us, before meeting you I did not even think that such a beautiful day will come in my life, that too soon.
"Meaning only the day is beautiful and not me?" I jokingly grinned.
Karan said- Hey Babu, you are the most beautiful in this world, this is like shaking open and flying hair, so sweet and big eyes… I feel like looking at them, this soft cheek, this ruddy red Lips, shining like silk, white body like milk, these big round boobs, these

full soft thighs and the way to go to heaven! It
seems that God has worked hard to make you.

Now I was not expecting such a compliment, then I
started looking under Smile Sharma.

Karan said on this - when you bow down Sharma's
eyes from above, you get so much love that just fills
in the arms and never leaves.
I got up and went to him and said - So don't fill it in
the arms… Who has stopped me?
And Karan held me tight in his arms.

Our bodies started getting hot as we came in
contact with each other and we started getting lost
in the trance of lust. We both had our eyes closed
and hugged and were enjoying each other's body
with body.
I opened my eyes and looked at Karan, Karan said
- when you look at these beautiful eyes with such
love, it seems that this world stops here and I
drown in them.

I had become emotional and maybe a couple of
tears in my eye.
Karan said - Hey, what happened?
I said in a complaining tone- Look, you made me
cry!
And started looking down.

Karan raised my face to his side and put his lips on
my lips and we closed the eyes and started kissing
Ummah…. Slowly the kiss went deeper and deeper
and I was being sucked up and down Karan's lips
by the wall, and that was mine.

By now one of Karan's hands was rubbing my
boobs and every one of my hands had reached his
dick. I slowly spread my palm and was rubbing her
upside down and she was getting excited. The
voices of Umm… Umm… Mmmh… to kiss both of
us were coming out loud in the room.

Karan brought me to the bed of Push, and we both
fell on the bed. Karan was kissing me like a goth
and kissing on every part of my body. I was
agonizing like a fish with his kiss.

Now Karan put his finger in my pussy and started
shaking and I started filling with joy. I was doing
Ummh… ehhh… hhhh… yah… in a dull voice.

In a while, my pussy was smooth and was yearning
to take the cock. I told Karan - what are you waiting
for now, do not put your cock.
Karan said - will not be in the mouth this time?
So I said - you pour it, man, I am not stopping.
Karan said- Good Baba, I will add a minute!

Then he got up and went to get the oil, brought a bottle of oil to lubricate his cock and said - now okay, what should I put?
I said - it was not needed, the pussy is very smooth, you just put it.

Karan set the latte on my pussy and bent over me. I was looking into her eyes and yes, I was begging to bend in a gesture of nodding. Karan applied a little push, because of the lubrication, the slipped slowly into the licked pussy and I slowly slid upwards while doing CEEE… CEEE… CEEE….

Initially, Karan was slowly putting the entire cock in and pulling out and I was lying in the bed with my eyes closed, ummah… mmmhh… ummah…. His cock was rubbing up against my g-spot, measuring the depth of my pussy and I was enjoying it very much.

Hmmmmm… hmmmmm… hmmmmm… while I was going to fuck with love and was being seen in my eyes.
When I looked up and down in the bed, I asked - what are you seeing?
Karan said- I see that a beautiful beautiful girl is lying naked in front of my eyes and my dick enters slowly by making space in her pussy and when she closes her eyes and takes so many alcoholic curses, then how beautiful It seems. Jannat is probably here.

I said - it is time for the pleasure of heaven, you
keep sexdai.

Now Karan had increased the speed slowly and I
was doing very fast while doing ahhhhhhhh. After
about 5 minutes, Karan's breath began to swell,
and he started loudly crying
I said - if you are tired then take a rest.
So he came next to me and fell.

Both of us turned towards each other and looked
into each other's eyes and started talking, as well
as I was rubbing her dick and she was moving my
body, never taking my hands off my boobs. It took
me to my waist and then to my ass.

When I started having some batch, I said what are
you doing?
Karan said - Come on Suhani, let's try from behind
today.
I thought of my forehead, you said- you mean you
want to fuck me from behind?

He nodded yes with a devilish smile.
I said no man, take as much as you want from the
front, but do not please from the back.
Karan said- Look, if you do not have the mind, then
I will not insist, but you can try once, please, for me,
we can try everything. You said that today I can ask
for anything...

I got up and sat down and said, man, you don't
understand, it hurts a lot from behind.
Karan said - how do you know it hurts? Have you
had it done before?

Now I could not tell him about Harshil, then I said -
No man, Tanvi had told.
Karan said - Hey why are you afraid, I will not let
you have pain, please please please!
And Karan now started persecuting a lot.

I was rubbing her cock and she was turning her
hands on my body, never taking my hands off my
boobs on my waist and then on my ass.
Karan said - Come on Suhani, let's try from behind
today.
I thought of my forehead, you said- you mean you
want to fuck me from behind? It hurts a lot from the
back.

Karan started persecuting a lot, so finally, I had to
bow down to his stubbornness and I said - take
good Baba Chod, happy?
Karan stood up completely and said - bow down
again!
I said - how to bend like this, first smooth it with oil,
there is no lubrication in the ass, and lubricate your
London too, then I will put it, otherwise no! Now I
obeyed so much, let me accept one thing as well.

Karan said- Come, Babu, I can only do so much for you. Let's lean forward.

I leaned forward on the bed and became a mare and handed her pussy and ass.
Karan said- Do this in such a way that you turn your face to the mirror so that I can see this beautiful face of you while fucking.
So I turned to the glass and started looking at both of us.

Now I was going to have painful sex once again in a while. Karan started massaging my ass with oil with his hands.
I said - Pour oil in… there will be more need.
He said - Okay, open the legs.
I opened it a little bit. My ass hole now opened slightly.

Karan then dabbed his finger in oil and placed it on my ass. As soon as he put a little finger in, I turned in front of Machal while doing Oui… cee… and said - Easy!
He said - okay dear!
And she started applying oil to the entire ass and prepared herself mentally to tolerate unbearable pain.

Karan said - Madam your mother and my cock are ready too, should I start?

I turned to face Karan and said - okay… but rest
easy, not like the wilderness.
He said- absolutely dear!

I turned my head back to the mirror and started
looking at both of us. Karan looked very happy as if
a small child had found his favourite toy, now he
just wanted to play with that toy.

Karan put the thick supra of his dick on my ass
hole, so I took a deep breath. As soon as Karan
penetrated his dick's mouth, I got a slight pain, so
my mouth opened and opened and came out and
the voice moved a bit.
I said - easy, easy… no hurry.
Karan said- Okay!

And then started trying to push slowly, then his dick
forcefully started making inroads into my ass.
Karan was also having trouble putting the dick, so
he too was pushing hard, hmm… on his dick and I
was crying my eyes out of pain.

Seeing this, Karan does not know whether the
ghost climbed with his full strength of my waist and
took his dick in my ass in one stroke, and I lean
forward on the bed with loud ahhh ummm…
Ahhh… Ahhh… Yeah… Aaaaaaaaa She went.
Karan was looking at me like this in a mirror.

At that time, he was not the one whom I loved, at
that time he was a devil of sex and I was a slave on
which he was being run over by his dick hunter.
Karan said - Do not get up, let Chodne properly.
I felt bad calling him like this ... but I got up and
became a mare.

Now Karan started fucking hard in my ass and I
kept on looking at both of us in the mirror. My ass
was hurting a lot but maybe I was sadder due to
being emotional, and 2-3 tears came from my eyes.
But I did not stop her and kept on fucking in the
ass.

I turned my head towards Karan and said - Ok
Chod Bhosdi… Chod as much as you can! If this is
so, I see how much power is there.
On hearing this, as if petrol had fallen in the fire of
Karan's lust, he said - take it again!
And he pulled out the whole dick and put it back
again and again and again after putting out the
whole dick, he started hitting back and forth in the
ass and hmm… hmm… sunnah… unnah….
I started shaking with her loud bumps, my whole
body, my hard boobs, hair, earrings were all
shaking loudly and I opened my mouth ahhhh…
ahh… ahh… ahhh… and from which… ahhh…
ahhh… My eyes were also filled with pain from time
to time.

Karan's dick was really long and thick, so stiff from above, which was stirring up the walls of the pussy. Slowly I started to enjoy it too and I started fucking very loud noises, I spoke - faster and faster.

But Karan was getting tired then he was fucking slowly. But I was hot and wanted Karan and Teja Chode.

Karan stopped and got out and sat on the side of the dick, I said - what happened, has it become a hobby or something else to do?
Karan said - Stop your sister's car... I tear your ass now, let me breathe and then see.

I sat down with my legs hanging from the bed and started watching her panting and also started slacking myself. Karan's dick was still flapping up and down.
I said to Karan - now you will get Chod or just do it.

Karan got excited and opened my legs with the feet of Lita on the bed holding me by the feet. So I could understand something and look up, Karan got into my ass again by lashing out.
I filled out a loud
aaaaaaaaaaaaaaaaahhhhhhhhhhhh ..

Karan, with all his strength, hmm… hmm… hmm… my ass started screaming loudly and I too was coming out loud. Karan, as if the train was being

made, I was going to shake it all and I was just
looking at the mirror.

Like this after fucking for 2-3 minutes, I told Karan -
wait… wait a minute!
Karan said - what happened? What broke you in
getting killed? She was speaking a lot.

I said - take the fuck later in the ass, first take the
fuck in the pussy, otherwise you will fall in the ass,
then you will not get the fuck and my fuck will be
incomplete.
Karan said - Alright!
And Karan removed the dick and put it in her pussy
and started pressing it.

Karan was bent over me and we both started
looking at each other's eyes. Now both of us were
getting up and down together and I was sighing…
Ahhh… Ahhh….
In between, both of us were rubbing lips with lips
while kissing each other out loud.

And after 3-4 minutes, the time of my loss started
coming, I even touched the sheet with my fist and
my voices started to stop, ahhh… ahhh… ahh…
ah… ahh… ahhh… and louder and louder… From,
please… and faster… and faster… sigh… come…
come…
And finally, shouting 'Aaa
aaaaaaaaaaaaaaaaaaaahhhhhhhhhhhhhhhhhhhhhh

hhhhhhhhhhhhhhhhhhhhhhhhhhhhhhhhhhhhhhhhh
hhhhhhhhhhhhhhhhhhhhhhhhhhhhhhhhhhhhhhhhhh
hhhh..?

My hand's fist also opened and I closed my eyes
and started breathing heavily. Karan took out the
dick and left me for a while and stood up.

After about a minute, when my breathing became
normal, I saw that Karan was watching me with
great love, like a naked fish lying on the bed.
Karan was stroking his dick and he was still in his
full enthusiasm.

I jokingly told Karan - I am done, now you shake it
off.
On this, Karan said to me - take this good sister!
And he held me in the legs and turned around so I
started laughing loudly… and started laughing
happily.

Karan smiled and grabbed me by the waist and
made a mare. I had understood that Karan would
fight only in the ass.
I still pretended to be unknown and said- Oh hey…
what are you doing?
Karan said- I will tell you now, sweetheart!

And Karan started trying to put cocks in my ass, but
due to the lubricity of oil, his cock started sliding out
again and again.

I supported him and said - wait, wait!
And took his head from bed to Teeka's hand on
ass, and with both hands widened the ass hole and
said- Now pour it.

Karan placed his cock on my ass hole and I
brought my hand forward and became a mare
again.
Karan said thank you and after hitting a loud blow,
he inserted his entire dick into my ass.

His shock shook me all the way to the bed, so I
shouted loudly…. My head woke up with a jerk and
my hair hung on the bouncy waist.
Karan started banging loudly without any care for
me and I kept moving back and forth on the bed.

Now I was not feeling much pain and I kept choking
with fun while saying 'Ahhh … Ahhh … Aa … Ah.
Karan pulled my open hair behind the grip in my fist
and my head was jerked up and up. In the room
just my loud sigh… ahh… Karan… ahhh… Karan…
and fast baby… and fast… ahhh… the sound of the
sobbing voice was coming and I shook back and
forth on the bed with the bumps of his dick. Was
living

Karan was going to fuck my ass like an animal,
hmm… hmm… ummah… ummah…. Karan was
also saying 'Ah… Suhani… Ah… Ahh Suhani…

Meri Jaan… Ye Le' and the Patta Patta were being
hit.

After fucking for 2-3 minutes like this, Karan started
fucking faster with the remaining strength.
I understood that now it is going to fall as well, so I
was also hitting her thighs while walking back and
forth on the bed, ahhh… ahh… aaa… ahhhh.

In a while, Karan stopped immediately and
snapped…. After that, while slowly beating 2-3
jerks, I filled the remaining semen in my ass and
pushed me forward.
I fell face down on the bed and started to gasp out
loud.

Karan too fell straight next to me, looking towards
the roof and opened his mouth and started panting
after him.

After a while I asked him - Are you happy now?
Karan looked at me and gave me a lovely kiss on
the lips and said - Yes, honey, I love you very
much.
I also smiled and said - I love you two.

I put a finger on the ass hole and saw it was all wet
and sticky there. I said, you relax, I go to the
bathroom.

As soon as I got up and started walking, drops of Karan's semen started dripping from my ass on the floor. Putting my hand on my ass, I entered the bathroom fast and sat on the commode.
Karan's semen was flowing from my ass. I forcefully threw out all the semen. I cleaned myself under the shower and sat on the floor and cleaned my pussy and ass as well.

When I returned to the room, Karan went to the bathroom to clean himself and I came naked and lay down on the bed.

In a while, Karan also came and lay naked next to me and said - Thank you, Janu.
I said - no problem!
And Karan took his side on me and put his leg on me and we did not know when we slept.

Tanvi's call in the morning opened my eyes. I told him - I will not be able to come to college today, you go away.
Tanvi said- seems to be freezing all night?
I said yes man… Karan has worsened the condition of Chod Chod. Come on, I will tell you all now, let me sleep now.

Karan was still sleeping with me in his arms and I slept again, hiding my head in his chest.

Infidelity to a lust-stricken husband

As soon as college was over, my father thought of getting me married, I didn't even get a chance to speak anything. I came to see a boy, Nitin liked me too. Nitin, the bank officer, was handsome in appearance and used to make things sweet. He had his home in a nearby town, his mother and father farming in the village.

I was going to miss my fun with Khurana Uncle, but that fun was going to meet me rightfully. Anyway, uncle and my relations were illegitimate, if anyone ever comes to know, then he is not able to show his face.

After two months my wedding date came out, and Uncle was very sad. But I celebrated them in a different way, on the day of engagement, I left the house by saying 'health is bad' and everyone came home till Uncle and we did around in the engagement sari.

I was screaming deliberately on the honeymoon, cutting with a blade on the foot and also putting

blood on the bed. Nitin did not suspect anything
from the red mehndi on the feet.

Gradually I got busy with my housework, in-laws,
in-law, in-between, pressing for grandchildren, but
my age was twenty-two years and Nitin was
twenty-five years old. Our married life and sex life
were also going well.

During Diwali, I went to my maternal uncle with my
husband, then I came to know that Khurana Uncle's
transfer has gone to another city. Now I relapsed,
that chapter was closed to me forever.

I would get up early in the morning, make Nitin a
tiffin. After Nitin left for office, she would finish her
household chores, do some exercise and yoga for
fitness, rest the rest of the time and then prepare
for dinner.
Relaxation resulted directly in my figure, but due to
yoga and exercise, I started looking more sexy.

Both of us were at home, so it used to be
mischievous, kissing each other, caressing delicate
organs or kissing and kissing.
But Nitin was a little shy and took less initiative.
Nitin did not even touch me among the people. But
when we were in the bedroom, he would make
every effort to satisfy me.

Nitin's sex was always simple and calm and sometimes boring, I did not want to hurt him by telling him nor did I want to cheat him. Sometimes I used to remember Khurana Uncle, I would remember his wild sex, then he would leave the water, then that night he would take the initiative to provoke Nitin and make our sex fun.

One day Nitin was to go to another branch of the office for three days for training. My periods started a day before leaving, so we could not have sex with our Happy Journey. Nitin came back when my periods were over, but he was very tired so he fell asleep early.

The next day was Saturday, so Nitin was going to come home in the afternoon. I also got ready to take a good bath, washed all the clothes to wear at home and wore only a gown on my bra panty. It was the rainy season outside, sitting in the hall looking at Nitin's path, going into the bedroom, doing sexy mischief, dreaming of taking four to five days' cancer.

The doorbell rang so I opened the door while running, Nitin came in, so I hugged him tightly.

"How long have you been… looking at your path since long." Nitin was a little shocked by this behaviour of me, pushing me away and he opened the whole door.

When I looked outside, two more people were standing and smiling at me, I felt very embarrassed.

Both of them were Nitin's cousins, Nitin made them both aware that they were standing a bit away from Nitin.

"These are my cousins, where I was training, they work right there. This is Amit and this Yuvraj, we met in training, both were going to return this evening, so brought them home to rest, said, have some tea, have breakfast, they will drop you at the airport. "

I called them in, sat on the couch and gave them water, both were almost Nitin's age.
"Sorry Bhabiji… Troubled you." Amit said.
"Otherwise… what trouble!" After speaking, I went to the kitchen, Nitin started talking to him.

After a while the doorbell rang, Nitin opened the door and there were people from the society. Someone was killed in society and Nitin was the secretary of the society, so he needed to stay there.
He came in and told me - I have to go to Argentina, I will come after 3-4 hours. Till then you give company to both of them.

I was very angry that everyone had put together my romantic mood. If I had guests at home, I could not

even vent my anger on Nitin. I made them
breakfast and kept doing odd jobs in the kitchen.
What would she say if she did not even know him!
Anyway, there was a fire inside the chat, she could
not even finger in the bathroom, what she had seen
would have made her suspicious.

After a while I brought tea for them, started picking
up the breakfast plate, then accidentally fell out of
my hand and broke. I got more angry, I went inside
and took the broom, collected all the big pieces of
plate and started collecting small pieces from the
towel.

While sitting and doing all this work, suddenly my
attention went to both of them, both were tearing
eyes and looking at me. Then I thought that maybe
they could see my breasts from the neck of the
gown, I was more embarrassed and went to the
kitchen from there.

Then clouds started thundering and stormy rains
started, I forgot everything and was watching the
beauty of nature from the kitchen window.
Suddenly I remembered that clothes have spread
to dry in the balcony of the hall. I went there on the
run, all the dry clothes got wet again due to rain. I
folded all the clothes one by one in the bucket, I
was completely drenched.

Removing water from my face, I came inside the hall, Amit and Yuvraj were watching me. Then I realized that I only wore the gown over the bra and panties, the white gown had become almost transparent with wetness and the clothes inside were easy to see.

I rushed towards the bedroom in shame, one Nitin is not at home… this rainy season… and these two men!

I went to the bedroom and closed the door, removed the soaked gown, removed the soaked bra panty and became completely naked. I was looking for my sari and blouse.

Then I felt the movement at the door, the light coming from under the door caught the sensation of someone being outside. My heartbeat with fear… I was naked in the house and alone and two men outside!

I felt scared for a moment… but a different sensation started coming in my mind. I remembered my and Khurana Uncle's stolen sex and I was thrilled. I thought of instigating them both. Not having a single cloth on my body, I stood in front of the door and took a sensual girdle in such a way that it appeared out of the door crack. Taking long stretches, I did a good job of my curvy breasts, flat stomach, vagina, and stuffed thighs, then showed me my round ass while taking down the blouse.

Then I wore an old blouse which was tightening me, bra panties were soaked, so I only wore a petticoat and wrapped the sari on top of the door. Then I stood near the door and started listening to them.

"Kya mast boobschhe hai saali ke..." Yuvraj said. "boobsche… what a complete product." Amit said- Nitin is also destined… Has a cool item been found.

Do not know why… instead of getting angry hearing these dirty things of mine, my pussy started getting wet. My nipples were also erect and the breasts also swollen. If Nitin was at home at this time, he would pounce on her like a lioness!
But what the hell… He was away from work.

Frustrated, I opened the door. But it took so much time for both of them to go back to the hall and sit at their place.

I went to the hall and asked them - liked it?
"what?" They both had faces at twelve o'clock.
I mischievously said laughing towards them - did you like the tea snack or not?
I have changed their mind as soon as they understand it.

"Wow… sister-in-law… was absolutely cool." Amit said with a laugh.
"And it was absolutely bitter… meaning tea… it was hard." Yuvraj said.

His double meaning words aroused the lust within me. But my mind was not ready to betray Nitin.

His condition was also similar. One, I got married… His cousin's wife, how would I react, it was difficult for him to guess, so he too was sitting with restlessness.

When I bowed down to pick up the cup of tea, my pallu ducked and slid down the shoulder, with the cup in my hands and I could not react quickly. More than half of my breasts were visible in tight blouses and were desperate to get out.
I stood in the same state of shock.

Nitin quickly moved forward and said - Bhabi, I catch them, you…
I gave the cups in his hands and while stealing sight of them, he corrected the sari's pallu. I did not even care about the cup of tea and I went to the kitchen in the same way, my heartbeat had now intensified, I could not understand what was happening.

I was standing near the kitchen table with my eyes closed, I felt someone from inside come inside the kitchen. Then came the sound of placing the cup of tea on the table, but I did not dare to open it.

then suddenly …A hand came over my shoulder, I turned backwards in fear and collided with Amit standing behind.
"Sister-in-law…" He removed his shoulder and brought me to my waist and pulled me closer.

I too did not retaliate with sexuality, he turned me on and held me in his arms. His hands fell on my breasts, and since when has the lust of suppressed lust exploded inside me, like a hungry person, we started kissing each other.

Amit used his experience to put his tongue in my mouth, now the tongue of the two of us was duelling with each other. She easily found my nipple inside the thin blouse and started rubbing it. I too was forgetting everything and putting a necklace around her neck and kissing her after forgetting everything.

Suddenly a touch of something hard was felt on my buttock. Yuvraj was standing behind and rubbing his erect cock on my butt. He started kissing me on the back of my neck and the open space on my back.
The fire inside me flared up more and I held Amit more tightly. On getting the green light from my

side, they also got excited and they started
mashing my delicate parts harder.
Yuvraj sat down and started to kiss my thighs by
putting my sari up, then Amit dropped my pallu and
rubbed my breast. With this double attack, I started
being a fool.
"Sss… ah…" My hospitality was filling them with
more vigour.

The prince had put my sari and petticoat up to the
waist. There was no panty inside, so my buttocks
were naked in front of him, Nitin was pressing them
with pleasure, kissing them on the balls and cutting
them with teeth.

"Sister… Slow… Don't cut…"
"Sorry sister-in-law ... your village ... your hips ...
you are so perfect ... I am living that I can eat ... just
be straight ... look at your pussy ..."
"Not here… let's go to the bedroom". Amit said.

The way I was supporting Amit and did not stop
Yuvraj from caressing her ass, he did not consider
it necessary to ask for my consent.

Both of them left me, then I got a chance to breathe
freely. But Amit was excited with lust, he pulled me
close and lifted me in the lap and started going
towards the bedroom. Amit kissed me in the
middle, Yuvraj started walking back, he was not

getting any chance, he was pressing my breasts as much as possible.

Both of them were in a hurry to consume me, seeing their sexuality, their rapture, I started laughing.

Amit made me stand near the bed and started to control his bloated breath. Till then, Yuvraj grabbed my pallu and removed my sari. Now I was only in petticoats and blouses.

Nitin took the front of my Nitambo, he started rubbing my hips above the petticoat. At that time, Yuvraj tore my blouse with one stroke and separated it from my body. I tried to cover my big round boobs with both my hands and removed my hands from my petticoat.

Amit took advantage of this and pulled the pulse of my Petticoat and then my Petticoat fell to the ground below.

Yuvraj then took off all his clothes and threw them away. His body was a gymnast and his cock was standing and moving between the legs. I kept looking at him and he started coming closer to me. He hugged me from the front and his cock started banging on my stomach.

Amit also took off all his clothes and started to clean his hands on my bare round hips from behind, in the middle he would try to touch my pussy but I was not even letting him reach thereby touching my thighs.

Yuvraj took care of my breasts and started sucking them alternately. He was holding my hands vigorously with both his hands. I was under attack from both sides and I was not getting a chance to retaliate.

Yuvraj would suck my right nipple, then kiss the valley between the breasts, hold the left nipple in the mouth, on the other side Amit was kissing my feet. Starting from the knees, he kept kissing up to the thighs and then started moving towards my pussy.
He lightly hit a kiss on my pussy, then my Rome was ruined.

"Ah… sister-in-law ... how sexy are you…" Amit said, clutching my legs in his arms.
Amit's body was also hard, he had thick black hair on his chest and back.

I was standing naked between those two naked men. Amit now stood up and clung to me from behind. His chest hair was tickling on my back and his weapon was trying to penetrate my ass crack.

Both of them were stroking my body as soon as I
got a chance.
My protest was now stopped. I felt the pleasure of
closing my eyes between two strong men.

"Come on, Amit quickly does around… If Nitin
comes, then there will be trouble." Yuvraj said and
we all became conscious.
Together they both picked me up and lay on the
bed.

Now Yuvraj came between my legs and inserted
his finger in the hidden pussy in my hair.
"Ssshh ... ahh ... slowly ..." Yuvraj was fast
fingerling in the pussy and my excitement was
reaching its peak.

Amit sat near my mouth and brought his cock near
my mouth- sister-in-law… please suck once!
His cock was quite long and thick. Seeing her big
pink betel nut, my mouth was watering. But I was
not going to show my rapture to him, I just did a
little kiss on his cock.

"Not like a sister-in-law… suck it right!" Amit started
trying to get his cock in my mouth.
I started taking half of his cock in the mouth,
showing compulsion.

At the bottom, Yuvraj removed his fingers from my
pussy and put his mouth on the pussy. I would

jump when his tongue hit my pussy. Amit was lovingly licking his cock with me while kneading my butt. No matter how much I tried to hide my excitement, my flowing pussy was doing everything.

Amit had licked all his cocks in my mouth and made my breasts red. Yuvraj filled my heart and drank my pussy juice and stood up. His black serpent was standing and drooling between his thighs.

"Amit ... Now I am not going ... I am going to put in law now ... sister-in-law, you become a mare." He was giving me spades like his wife.
In lust, I had become a puppet in their hands and was obeying everything.

Amit now sat back on the headrest of our king size bed and told me to be a mare in front of me. His cock was right in front of me. He grabbed my head and put it in my mouth, Yuvraj came behind me and sat down on his knees and rubbed his cock on my ass.

My pussy was completely wet, I was now waiting to enter inside the cocks as a batsman with lust.

Yuvraj got a sense of wetness by putting a finger in my pussy, adjusting the height of my ass, he put his cock on the crack of my pussy and in one stroke, it

was completely inside. Amit's cock was full of my mouth so I could not even scream.
"Yuvraj… man… slowly, my cock will get teeth." Amit said.
"Will you have teeth?" My pain did not bother both of them, so I intentionally cut his cock lightly.
"Ah… no sister-in-law… we will do it slowly…" Amit said groaning painfully.

Yuvraj's car had caught his speed behind him, bowing down, he was fucking me with his hands, mumming me while hanging. My lust was also at the peak, I was also backing my waist and supporting her.

Amit removed my mouth from his cock and said to the prince - brother-in-law, he is applying alone… But now I want to fuck.
Saying this, Amit slipped down and came down to me.

On the other hand, Yuvraj took his cock out of my pussy and I woke up. I quickly climbed down lying on top of Amit and started rubbing my pussy on his cock. I put my hand down and set Amit's cock on the crack of the pussy and slowly started taking it inside her pussy while going down.

Amit bowed me forward and started sucking my boobs with fun lying down. I started jumping on his cock while shaking my waist. Amit was also raising his waist from below and was fucking me. Kissing hands on my breasts, thighs, ass on waist, I was not even aware, I was enjoying the fuck with my eyes closed.

"Sister-in-law ... I'm going to be." Sucking my breasts brutally, Amit shouted while stroking and started banging fast.
I had also fallen twice and was enjoying the fast cocks in the pussy.

Amit applied me tightly to the chest and started to release his water in my pussy while closing my lips with his lips. Due to the warmth of her semen, I once again collapsed. I lay on her body for a while, Amit was kissing me while rubbing my back.

Yuvraj was standing shaking his cock with restlessness, after Amit's presence, he too started showing haste.
"Amit bhai ... shun away ... tera ho gaya na ... Nitin comes, then I will be hungry." Yuvraj climbed on top of the bed.
"Look Bhabhi, how desperate you are to get inside my pussy..." He started pressing my boobs and kissing on the back.

Seeing his rapture, I laughed at myself, I got up from Amit. His cock was now loose and easily came out of the pussy.

With that, the work of both of us came out and started flowing down the thighs.

I moved on top of Amit and lay down on his back, Yuvraj came between my thighs, running on my knees and started rubbing cocks on my pussy, spreading my legs. I laughed seeing his rapture.

"Hey wait… me… ass…" My smile remained in my throat, Yuvraj had penetrated my cock inside her pussy in one stroke.
"Sssss… Sister-in-law ... Someone will listen." Amit lying with me said while turning to my curfew.

Amit kissed my cheek and lips, started rubbing my nipple and stroking my breast. Yuvraj was excited, holding my thighs in his hands, Danadan was pushing.
Fearing Nitin's return, the excitement of fucking two men and Amit's caressing made my pussy ready to release water again.

Yuvraj had caught good speed, pressing his lips under his teeth and closing his eyes, he was pushing in a rhythm. I was also enjoying it, I grabbed Amit's head lying close to my face and started kissing him.

He was constantly being subjected to my breast, I put one hand down and put it on his cock. Amit's cock was starting to stand again, I started caressing his cock. Yuvraj also increased the speed of his bumps.

By the way, my pussy started going towards its peak, I removed my mouth from Amit's mouth and started shouting.
"Ah… young… ss raj… and sharp… mine… having… ah…" Hearing my sobbing voice, he got rid of his dam and he started dropping hot semen in my pussy. Yuvraj fell down on me calmly after putting 10 to 12 strikes in stormy speed.

I had forgotten the number of showers, how many times. We both stayed in each other's arms for a while. After a while, Yuvraj removed from my top and lay down, but I lay in the same position. After a long time, due to the tremendous sex I had, I was lethargic.

After a while, I woke up with a fist and saw Amit sitting between my legs, his cock was ready for the second round.

"No … not now … I'm tired … Nitin must become now too." I was refusing but where Amit was going to believe, he started trying to convince me by pressing my breast and kissing him - once sister-in-law… please down… if not then take it in mouth… please… once…

Seeing his erect penis, I also melted and while sleeping on my stomach, I started sucking his cock. Amit was standing under the bed, holding his head and putting his cock inside my mouth. Suddenly someone touched my ass, I looked behind me while sucking Amit's cock, then the prince was behind.

Yuvraj's cock was also ready again and he was rubbing his cock on my pussy from behind, I tried to say something till then Amit grabbed my head again and inserted his cock in my mouth till the root.

In my wet pussy, Yuvraj inserted his cock and started banging. The three of us were giving each other full satisfaction in the light of lust. Both were not taking the name of loss, I was enjoying the attack on both sides, water was being released.

Finally, both of them came close to the car, Amit's cock started fluttering in my mouth. Amit took his cock out of his mouth and started shaking it fast with his hands, then started staring at the mouth and dropping semen in my mouth.

The state of Yuvraj was also like this, he also took out his cock and left his water on my ass.

The three of us were very tired and lay on the bed, the sound of loud breaths echoing in the room.

After a while both got up and started wearing
clothes, I also got up and went to the bathroom and
took a good shower. Just when the towels came
out wrapped, they saw both sitting in the hall
outside.

I quickly got out of the cupboard and put on another
sari, then cleaned the bedroom properly and
entered the hall. Nobody was talking to anyone.

Later Amit came to me and told me while kissing -
Thank you Bhabhiji… We had such an experience
before… You are really so sexy…
Yuvraj also came to me and kissed me.

Then the doorbell rang and the three of us came to
our senses, opening the door and saw that Nitin
had come.

I did not talk to him and went straight to the
bedroom and slept.
Nitin talked to both of them for a while and went to
leave them at the airport.

As soon as it was dark, I woke up and made food,
Nitin was sad to betray her husband but more than
that it was a pleasure to fuck. I ate food and fell
asleep again.
When Nitin returned at night, I did not talk to him,
he felt that I was angry and he also fell asleep.

The second day everything became normal and we again started living like Raja Rani.

Fifty years hard cock

I am Anand Mehta, fifty years old. I am writing this Chodan story for you dear readers. Hope you enjoy reading it.

I live in a rented house. The house above me houses the landlord's family, in which a beautiful married girl lives with her 5-year-old daughter. Her 30-year-old husband is employed as a teacher in a 10 + 2 school in another district, so he comes home only during the holidays.

It was only a month before I came to this new house that I got to see the real appearance of the landlady.

One day I was going to the house above to pay my house rent. When we reached near the door, there were very slow murmurs and moaning sounds. I am a fifty-year-old man. Hearing these voices, I remembered the euphoria celebrated with my wife. On that day, I put my full strength of 26 years on

the newly-wedded wife. She went limp for four
days.
Whenever I think about that day, sensual vibrations
start happening in the whole body.

I came out of these memories when 5000 rupee
notes held in my hands fell.
I started to feel that the landlord is definitely having
sex with someone.

Still, my heart was not accepting this, her husband
is outside in another district, so who is inside?

I gently tugged the side window of the balcony.
Oh God! What is going on? Two strong men were
having fun with the landlady. She was lying on the
bed and was repeatedly filling hers. A fat man from
above, with his big belly, was climbing on that poor
thing and his cocks were being moved in and out
while up and down.

The second fat man was rubbing the poor woman's
pussy with one hand and stroking his erect penis
with his other hand. The man who rubbed the
cucumber was the rogue leader of my region when
I looked at him carefully, I came to know.

Man will probably be his friend.

I started abusing the leader in my mind 'Sala!
fucker! The fieldwork does not work properly and

coming here, it is being given a very good
treatment on its erect cocks. '

My attention went to that girl. Ah… ah… Seeing her
bare body was on fire in my body. He was trying to
mash his two big boobs with his hands. My hair
was aroused by her naked body.

Now the leader's turn to fuck His stomach was too
much protruding. He started fucking the girl as a
bitch. The leader was being pushed from behind
and the mistress was moaning in pain.

My eyes were enjoying seeing her two Tits hanging
down. I was yearning to take his naked body in my
arms and my cock to go to his bur. My cock started
whipping to get out and it was full.

I opened the chain of my pants and pulled my hard
long cocks with my hand and pulled them out.
Water came out of my cock.
I said to myself, 'One day you must surely fuck me!
Otherwise, my name is not Anand Mehta.

After looking at her bare body, I closed my eyes
and started caressing and licking my long-standing
cocks, imagining that girl fucking. After about ten
minutes the juice started coming out of my cock.

Even after getting the juice out of my cock, my cock
did not come as normal. Was still yearning to enter

his bur. Seeing her naked body again, I started to mutter loudly.

This time a lot of juice came out and after some time I started feeling a little relieved. I opened my cock inside the pants and started going back to my house without paying any rent.

Reached his house and sat on the couch. Then my wife came and grabbed my shoulder and shook and said - Where are you lost? Don't have to go to the office?

In my mind, just thinking about fucking him. In my dreams, I was putting my hand fingers in and out of his bur. How much fun it was… uh… uh… her sobbing voice.

My wife also interfered in dreaming. Can not a man fuck a young girl even in his dreams?

Coming out of these dreams, I said - No ma'am! Will not go to the office, it looks like a lot of weakness right now.

She said - but until some time ago you were feeling fine, now what happened?

I said - Hey Madam! The disease can happen anywhere, anytime… especially heart disease.

She became silent after I spoke.

When I looked at my wife's face, she was seeing the bulge between my two legs. Then she came

and sat beside me, looking at my face with
suspicion.
I panicked… I understand that my theft has been
caught.

Touching the pants on top of my bulging cocks,
quote - here it is wet… You went to pay the rent
didn't you? Is Mistress coming to Chod?
I quickly backed away and said- Hey! What are you
saying… I will fuck my mistress… No, it is not.
I said in my mind 'What kind of wife I have got… I
do not understand the work and what is not
supposed to be understood… Oops!'

The wife again asked - So tell me, how wet there?
I said with some anger - If you want to hear the
truth, then listen. You are busy in bhajan and pooja
day and night… It has been a full month, having
sex with you… You do not give… My penis was
standing today… There was only one way to calm it
down. Muth kar 'What happened in it when I killed
it.

My wife said a little hesitantly- I don't feel like
having sex anymore… Why don't you find someone
else to calm your sex… I will not say anything to
you.
I happily spoke - true darling! Are you not joking?

She said with a sense of wisdom the second time -
you are so happy. Is anyone already looking for
them?
I immediately spoke - Yes… Mistress above.
She said in surprise - what a young lady! Will that
girl be able to bear the shock of your fat cock? You
will tear his evil, as he used to do with me earlier.

I hugged my wife with my arms and said - it is her
job to bear my cock. Let everyone like you get a
wife who gives free leave to her husband, thinks
about her husband.

That night, I got the landlady in my dream, and I
had a dream in the night, due to which my worn
lungi was smelling a lot in the morning.
As soon as waking up in the morning, the first
thought came to fuck that prostitute. The
prostitute's naked blonde body floated before my
eyes. From now on, my black cock stood up and
came out of the lungi.

I do not wear undergarments at night… In the
daytime, my penis remains tight inside the panties,
so at night it relaxes.

When the wife came to give tea, her eyes first went
to my erect cocks instead of my face, she was a
little shocked and said while holding tea - you are
fifty years old, yet your penis is always hot… your
black banana is absolutely Still completely young.

I also paid attention to my moustache and then holding my black banana in my hand, while looking at my wife, said - this is Anand Mehta's cock… until it gives it to the prostitute, it will not calm down…
See you How my cock is killing like a snake… Now just get a bill.
Biwi bid - still have to go to the office or not?
I rubbed the cocks with one hand and said - No… I have taken leave for three days.

After about an hour I started going upstairs wearing a shirt and a new lungi with the rental money.
Reached near the landlady's house and rang the bell.
He opened the door and on seeing me said - Hey Mehta Ji! Come, come to pay rent? Would have called me!

Hearing the words of his end, I said - yesterday I was thinking that I should call you at night but did not call.
She smiled a little. It seemed as if she had understood the true meaning of my double meaning.

Leaving that tone, he said - Yes, you will get free time in the night, you will stay in the office all day.
I sat on a couch and sat on the couch right in front of me. Her hair smelled of shampoo… She was just now in a red and white mixed design saree by

taking a bath. Her two ripe juicy mangoes were
visible from above her blouse. His thin waist was
hurting my heart.

I was just sitting on the couch when my cocks
started getting ready to wreak havoc… The blood
flow in my two big antlers and black bananas
hanging between the two legs started getting very
fast. I started taking money out of my shirt pocket.

When his soft fingers touched my fingers, as my
whole body caught fire and this fire was getting
excited by his dark red coloured saree.
She said- And tell me, how is your work going?
I said in a voluptuous tone - the work is going well,
just one work has stopped.
Handling the matter said - Factory work is a bit
tardy nowadays.

Both of us were talking that suddenly the mistress's
white-haired pet dog came near my feet and barked
and pulled my lungi with his teeth. This sudden
stretch opened the knot of my lungi and I saw black
stuff stored for fifty years.

I looked at the mistress… her eyes were looking at
my erect cocks.
I quickly hid it from lungi.
When the mistress rebuffed the dog, he went away.

I now stood up and started tightening my lungi
properly. The mistress's eyes still rested between
my two legs.

She stood up and came near me and started
caressing the lungi on top of my cock. A few
seconds later, I pressed my two big aunts hard. I
was taking deep breaths… I started having fun… I
thought of sucking her juicy lips that she put her lips
on my lips. I grabbed her face vigorously and
started to drink the juice of her juicy lips loudly.
After so many years, such juicy lips were found.

He put his hand inside the lungi and took out my
black banana and started to hold it back and forth.
Sometimes she even pressed my banana hard.

After a few minutes, she started removing the
bondage of my hands from her face. I removed my
hands from his face. She immediately sat down on
her knees and started sucking my standing
90-degree cocks in her mouth.
It seemed as if she was sucking some chocolate,
not cocks.

The sobbing voice started coming out of my mouth
- aa… aa… hah… huh… what's the matter…
having fun… and suck!
Half of my cock was not able to enter her mouth,
but when she rubbed her soft lips on the edge of
the hole, then what is the matter of that pleasure?

Sucked lips for fifteen minutes and through him my cock sucked.

Then I said - just my queen! Do you have to suck my cock or even fuck it?
Having said this, I picked him up and took him in my arms and started going towards a room. She was taking her left hand inside my shirt and rubbing the hair on my chest. I was awakened so much that I was thinking that I should give it a fuck only by placing it on the floor.

But ass is more fun to fuck on the bed, thinking that I reached the room and slammed him on the bed and started to open my shirt in excitement. She too began to open her sari. Opening the shirt and opening my lungi in one stroke… she was watching me unbuttoning her clothes.
Seeing me not wearing panties, he said - I had already come to arrange the fuck?
I said - you know now… My cock has been craving to go to your burrow since yesterday morning.

She was opening her blouse with a sari. I got naked and jumped on the bed and stood up. She wanted to say something that I put my black hard banana in her mouth. She then started sucking him.

I said while filling in with sobbing sound- I will do things after fucking the queen!

Oops… oops… my cock going in and out of her mouth… Anand had no limit.

I said - queen! This work should have been done long ago… oops… ah… ha… suck… suck my cock and blacken it.

Then lying on her bed, I quickly started to open her shadow. Saya opened but her inner panties were not opening. The panties were very tight.

She started laughing at my batch and said - Mehta Ji! Relax a little… so sensual and restless for fucking, my husband did not become even on a honeymoon as you are now!
Having said this, she opened her tight panties in a jolt and I put my fifty years old and stocky body on her bare body and started sucking her two big boobs in the mouth. If he used to press both of his boobs with his hands in between, he would get a groan from his mouth.

She was being caressed with my hands on my back and sometimes on my face. By now my cock had attained its maximum length.

I grabbed my cock with his right hand and brought it near his bur and in one stroke, he entered it. With each tremor, he screamed.

Initially, my whole cock was not going in… I said -
how many are you fucking, yet your evil is not
loose?
She spoke - I have not got such thick and long
cocks till date Mehta ji!
I said - no problem, it will be lost today.

Having said this, I put a lot of pressure… this time
my cock had gone deep inside. She started
groaning with pain and said- you tore me today.
Ummah… Ahh… Hah… Yah…

I continued my fucking work. After five, six shakes,
he too started to enjoy and started speaking -
Chodo… and Chodo.

After a few minutes she became a bitch and I beat
her pussy from behind. She loved fucked by being
a bitch. Then after about twenty minutes, I fell into it
while doing the sounds of Fachak-Fachak.

Eventually, the hot semen of my cock quench her
thirst.
She said thank you, Mehta! To reach me at the
peak of sex… never reached the peak point like
today.

And we both started slapping each other's arms.
The warmth of each other's bodies was making us
happy and giving us peace.